Diego de Granada

Argentina Palacios
Illustrated by Elizabeth Wolf

Rigby

Contents

Foreword

The story of Diego de Granada takes place in the first part of the 16th century. This was an exciting time for Spain. The journeys of Christopher Columbus began Spain's conquest of the West Indies and other parts of the New World.

Columbus was followed by other explorers who made their own voyages of discovery. By 1515, trade between Spain and the Indies was commonplace. Great fleets left the port of Seville twice a year, in the spring and in the fall. They returned loaded with precious cargo. By law, one-fifth of that cargo belonged to the king, which made Carlos, the king of Spain, rich indeed.

This wealth was enjoyed by others as well. Many merchants made great fortunes selling goods to those who were headed off to settle the lands of the New World. And investors who funded the ships shared in the treasures that were brought back.

Still, some people were very poor. Diego was one of them. Like so many others, he struggled to survive. Also like them, he dreamed of traveling to the New World where he could make a better life for himself.

This is his story.

I, Diego de Granada

I read every word on the page for a second time. To my satisfaction, there were still no errors to be found. I breathed a deep sigh of relief.

You may wonder at my concern. After all, most boys of 13 are not so fussy about the written word. However, I love words in any form—spoken, sung, shouted, scribbled, carefully hand-written, or printed on a printing press. But printed most of all.

Perhaps it is because I talk so much that the idea of capturing words on paper excites me. Perhaps it is because what I do now is so much better than what I have done in the past.

But I am getting ahead of myself. You do not know who I am or what my life has been like. So how can you understand why the job of printer's apprentice means so much to me?

My name is Diego de Granada and I live in Seville—to my way of thinking, the finest city in the entire kingdom of Spain. I am not alone in that opinion, either. An ancient saying states, "Who has not seen Seville, has not seen a wonder."

So why do I call myself Diego of Granada, you ask? It is not because I have a special fondness for Granada, the city of my birth. No, Seville is the city I love. I liked the word "Granada," that is all. I thought that it sounded important—at least at the time I began to call myself by the name. And now, it is simply who I am: Diego de Granada, printer's apprentice in Seville.

How did I get from Granada to Seville? From orphan to trusted apprentice? Ah, it is a tale of adventure and misadventure, of kindness and cruelty, of hope and disappointment. It is a tale I will tell you now.

My Most Terrible Fate

"Come along, boy," Tío Rodrigo said in a gruff voice. Without responding, I followed in his footsteps. My head was down to hide the tears that I could not hold back.

Though I called him by that name, Tío Rodrigo was not really my uncle. He had been a friend to my father for many years. They had both been mule drivers—until the day my father went off on a trip and never returned. He was killed in an accident. Nobody has ever learned exactly why or how it happened, but he fell from a mule's back and into a deep ravine. I was only two or three at the time, so I barely remember him.

After my father's death, my mother and I went from being somewhat poor to being desperately poor. It was extremely hard for a widow with a small child to make a living. Most of the time, she worked as a ragpicker. She walked from one end of Granada to the other, looking for discarded items. These she would fix and sell to others. Others who were almost as needy as we were.

When there was little to find, she resorted to begging. She would sit on the steps of one church or another, hoping those who worshipped there would take pity on her. She hated doing this, but we had to eat and keep some sort of roof over our heads.

There was never much on our table, but it was enough to keep us alive. We wore the same simple clothes year in and year out. In the summer we were too hot, and in the winter we were too cold; however, our bodies were always decently covered. Our roof often leaked when it rained, but fortunately in Granada there is more sunshine than rain. So despite our troubles, somehow we managed.

Out of love for my father, Tío Rodrigo tried to look out for my mother and me. But he was no richer than we, so there was little he could do. Still, he had been a constant presence in my life, visiting every month or so. My mother and I were always glad to see him.

Now, without slowing his steps, Tío Rodrigo broke the silence. "I am truly sorry, Diego. Your mother was a good woman. I regret that I did not arrive before she died. That I was not here with you."

I nodded, still not speaking. Tío Rodrigo knew I was upset, for he had rarely seen me quiet for so long. He understood, however. After all, my mother's death had been only three days earlier.

"I would take you with me if I could," Tío Rodrigo continued. "But the life of a mule driver is difficult. And you are such a puny thing, Diego. You would not last long, I fear."

"I am small, but I am strong," I protested, stung enough to speak. "I could be a help to you. And mules like me, Tío Rodrigo. They listen when I talk. They seem to like it when I tell them my stories."

Tío Rodrigo shook his head. "I am sorry, Diego," he said again. "Most days I make barely enough to feed myself. I cannot feed a growing boy as well. Now, cheer up. The orphanage will not be so terrible. You need a home, and it *is* a home. You will have food to eat and a roof to shelter you. There will be other boys there—many of them your age. And who knows, you might even learn a worthwhile trade. Perhaps you can look forward to being something more than a mule driver or a ragpicker."

I was in no condition to argue—or even to

offer an opinion. I was bewildered, confused, and hurting. I was only ten years old, and I was an orphan.

Even at this tender age, I knew that it was far better to be poor and have a parent than to be an orphan. But, as is so often true of misfortune, it was not really a matter of choice.

So I let Tío Rodrigo lead me to the "Home for Waifs." A waif is simply a high-sounding name for a homeless child. And since I was clearly homeless, and clearly a child, that is what I was. I did not like the sound of the word. I did not like much of anything that was happening to me.

"Here we are," said Tío Rodrigo some thirty minutes later. We had reached the outskirts of Granada, where the orphanage lay. Now it stood before us, two stories of gray stone rising from the cobblestoned street. A thick stone fence stretched out for some distance to either side of the building, hiding what lay beyond.

The orphanage was far more substantial than the rough shack where my mother and I had lived. It was also far less welcoming. The heavy wooden door was closed tightly, despite the fact that it was a bright and sunny day. I suspected that little sunshine was allowed to sneak inside these walls.

I watched wearily as Tío Rodrigo's work-roughened fist pounded on the door. Footsteps could be heard from inside. Then the hinges protested noisily and the door slowly swung open.

A tall, thin woman stood in the doorway. She was dressed in the severe, dark clothing of a nun. Her expression was as severe and dark as her robes.

"May I help you?"

Tío Rodrigo snatched his hat off and dipped his head respectfully. "I brought this boy to you," he said. "He is a good boy, Sister. His mother and father are both dead, and though I love him like a son, I cannot care for him myself."

The woman's eyes moved to my face. "What is your name, boy?" she asked. Her voice was stern, but not unkind.

"Diego," I answered in a whisper.

"And who were your parents?" she inquired. After I told her their names, she nodded. I am sure she did not know of them, but I liked it that she had asked. Saying the names of my mother and father made their memories more real to me.

The nun addressed Tío Rodrigo. "You have done the right thing by bringing the boy here," she said. "We can always find room for another needy child."

Then she turned to me. "Come, Diego, and I will show you around. My name is Sister Teresa."

There was time for only a hasty farewell. I am not ashamed to say that I cried. And for his part, Tío Rodrigo's eyes were filled with unshed tears.

Then he embraced me once and walked away without a backward glance. I stepped through the door of the orphanage, following Sister Teresa into my new home.

A large dining hall and kitchen took up most of the building's first floor. Off to the left was a door that Sister Teresa explained led to the nuns' living quarters. To the right was a steep wooden stairway. It led to the dormitory, where the orphans slept. That is where Sister Teresa took me.

The walls of the dormitory were lined with narrow beds—about a dozen on each side, if I remember correctly. I was left there in the charge of an ancient nun with a wrinkled face and thick, gray eyebrows. This woman, Sister Dora, was as short and plump as Sister Teresa was tall and thin.

The sister assigned me to a bed—the second from the end on the left side of the room. Then she gave me a change of clothes. I was grateful, as I had only dirty rags on my back. The clothing I received was hardly luxurious, but it was clean and neatly patched.

"Now, Diego," said Sister Dora after I was dressed, "there are things you need to know. We have rules and a schedule. Both must be followed. You will rise every morning at five o'clock. We all work hard here, both indoors and out. Right now, when it is summer, you will be working in the fields.

After all, if we do not work, we do not eat."

She went on to explain that we would have breakfast after working for several hours. Then it was back to work until the lunch bell rang. After lunch, it was time for lessons until dinner was served. Kitchen chores would occupy us until bedtime. Once the lights were out, there was to be no talking.

In between all these activities, there were frequent pauses for prayer. This was only natural, I suppose. After all, the nuns were women who had dedicated their lives to prayer and good works.

"And on no occasion is there to be any mischief of the kind boys seem to like so much," Sister Dora said in a no-nonsense voice. "Life here is serious business, Diego. There is no time for foolishness. And no patience for boys who choose to act in foolish ways."

I did not care about the hard work. And in my present mood, I had no thoughts of horseplay—or any other kind of play, for that matter. All that concerned me was knowing that I would have three meals a day and a place to lay my head at night.

I was not so sure about the lessons, however. After all, I had never gone to school. Learning was hardly an occupation for boys as poor as I had always been. I was not exactly sure how I felt about suddenly becoming a student. However, it seemed a small enough price to pay for a full stomach.

Sister Dora broke into my thoughts. "Diego? Are you listening to me? I have asked you twice if you understand the rules and the schedule. Do you?"

"Yes, Sister," I said hastily.

"Fine then," she said. "Now I will see that someone shows you where you will be working today. It is still an hour until lunch, so you may as well make yourself useful."

With that, Sister Dora marched out of the room, her heels tapping out a hollow tune on the floorboards. She did not look back, as if she clearly knew that I would do as she had said. I lost no time in following her.

And so my life as an orphan began.

Life as an Orphan

"Diego!"

Sister Ana's voice was loud enough to get my attention. But then, Sister Ana's voice was always loud. The sturdy nun was in charge of the fields and gardens of the orphanage. I think she shouted because she spent so much time with us outside, where we managed to stay out of earshot as much as possible.

"Did you finish feeding the hens and gathering the eggs?" she asked.

"I fed them, Sister," I answered in all honesty.

"Then where are the eggs, Diego?" she asked. "Did every hen decide not to lay for us today?"

"I forgot, Sister," I admitted. "I will go and gather them now."

"See that you do," she ordered with a deep sigh. It seemed that Sister Ana had been sighing ever since my arrival. Has she always been like this, or do I have something to do with it? I wondered.

I hurried back to the shed that housed the chickens. I did not like it there. The ceiling was low, even for a boy of my size. The smell was terrible. And the hens seemed equally stupid and mean. They pecked angrily at my hand whenever I reached under them for an egg.

Still, it had to be done. So I got through the chore as quickly as possible. Then, after checking with Sister Dora, I hurried back to the kitchen with the basket of eggs.

"Only three broken today, I see," said Doña Rosa, the village woman who was in charge of cooking for the orphanage. "That is an improvement, Diego. Perhaps tomorrow you can get *all* the eggs to me in good condition."

"Perhaps," I agreed. "Though they seem to break when I merely look at them."

Doña Rosa looked at my forlorn face and a smile creased her broad face. "Do not be so sad, Diego. After all, I have to break the eggs to use them. With you gathering them, I have no difficulty deciding which to use first."

I returned her smile, feeling more lighthearted. Doña Rosa had been most kind to me since my arrival. She seemed to feel sorry for me because I was so small and so thin. At least that is what I thought, since she sometimes slipped me something extra to eat, as she did now.

"Take this, Diego," she said, handing me a thick slice of bread still warm from the oven. "You need to put some meat on those bones."

I stuffed half the bread in my mouth as soon as I had finished expressing my gratitude. Then, clutching the other half in one hand, I left the kitchen.

The bread was a treat. I had quickly learned that although we truly did receive three meals a day, the portions were hardly generous and there was little variety to our fare. Bread with butter and cheese for breakfast, washed down with a swallow or two of milk. Bread and cheese and sometimes a piece of fruit for lunch. Dinner usually consisted of vegetables and more bread and, perhaps once a week, an egg. On Sundays, we might have a handful of olives as a special treat. And while I had heard that a morsel of meat or fish occasionally found its way to our plates, I had seen neither since my arrival. Needless to say, there were no plump orphans to be found in the Home for Waifs.

Once outside, I looked around carefully. I had been at the orphanage for less than ten days. It had only taken me one of the ten to learn which of my fellow orphans were best avoided. There was a group of boys who seemed to delight in making life miserable for those of us who were smaller and more timid.

"Diego!" someone shouted.

I felt my heart jerk wildly in my chest. The voice belonged to Bernardo, the leader of the tormentors. Yesterday he had snatched a chunk of cheese from my hand before I could take a single bite. Now, thinking only to guard my bread from his greedy fingers, I ran.

Heavy footsteps thundered behind me. I knew that Bernardo could overtake me easily. After all, his legs were half again as long as mine.

Acting on instinct, I went around a corner and ducked into the cowshed. There I took shelter behind a large milk cow.

To my relief, Bernardo ran past, still shouting my name. I slumped down into the dirty straw, breathing heavily and thanking the fates for sparing me.

"Diego? Is that you?"

The whispered inquiry startled me. Was I hearing things? Had the cows suddenly begun speaking?

"Here," the voice said, "behind you." I turned to look. A figure crouched there, covered with bits of straw and other things I did not care to name. It was Alonso, a boy about my age. We had hardly spoken since my arrival, but I had noticed him. His face usually bore the same worried expression that I suspected appeared on mine.

"What are you doing here?" I asked now.

"The same thing you are," he responded. "Trying to stay away from Bernardo."

"What does he want with us?" I asked.

"I don't know," admitted Alonso. "I was sure that whatever it was could not be pleasant, so I took off when he called my name."

I nodded, understanding how he felt. Then I looked at my hand. Doña Rosa's bread was a bit squashed, and there were a few bits of straw clinging to the crust. Still, it was edible. I broke the piece apart and offered half to Alonso.

"Thank you," he said with some surprise. Then we chewed companionably. We had just finished when the bells rang, announcing that it was lunchtime.

We waited until a band of boys walked by the shed. Then we slipped out and joined the stragglers in the group. To our relief, Bernardo was not among them. We would have to deal with him again, but at least it appeared we would be allowed to eat one more meal first.

The next morning I was assigned to work in the fields. These began behind the orphanage and extended all the way to the river like a blanket striped in shades of green. I cannot remember what river it was, but that does not matter to my story.

The fields were planted with cabbage, onions, spinach, radishes, and other vegetables. Some of these occasionally showed up on the dinner table, but most were sold in town to help support the orphanage.

When I reached the section of the field I was to weed, I was happy to see that Alonso was there as well. I was equally happy to see that Bernardo and his friends were nowhere in sight.

Alonso and I soon managed to work our way to rows that were next to one another. As we pulled weeds from around the tender plants, we talked in low voices.

"How long have you lived here?" I asked him at one point.

"As long as I can remember," answered Alonso with a shrug of his shoulders. "In fact, I do not recall living anywhere else. So I must have been very young when I first arrived."

I felt a pang of sorrow for him. At least I remembered something other than this. I remembered my mother. I could close my eyes and see her. I could hear her soft voice as she sang to me and told stories over and over so that now I could tell them to myself. For these memories, I was suddenly grateful beyond measure.

We went on to speak of other things. Of our likes and dislikes. And of our dreams and hopes. (Yes, even orphans can aspire to such things.)

"I want to be a beekeeper," Alonso confided.

I shuddered. I had not yet been assigned to work with the bees. I dreaded the possibility. As much as I liked the sweetness of honey, I wanted nothing to do with its production. Or with the creatures that produced it.

"Aren't you afraid you'll be stung?" I asked.

"Not really," he answered. "They leave you alone as long as you move slowly and do nothing to threaten them."

He went on to tell me about the hives that belonged to the orphanage. They were not close to where anyone lived, he said. That was to protect both bees and people. And all the flowers that bees liked grew nearby. So the creatures had no reason to abandon their hives and go elsewhere.

"What about you?" Alonso asked, once he had tired of talking of bees. "What trade do you hope to learn?"

"I do not know," I answered. And I truly did not. I knew I was not interested in beekeeping. Or in raising chickens, herding cows, or growing vegetables. The truth was that I found all these occupations extremely boring, even though I had only been at them for a matter of days.

"I once thought about being a mule driver, like my father," I said. "You can travel. And I like mules better than chickens or cows—or bees. But it is hard work and I fear I shall never be strong enough to do it."

Alonso nodded wisely. "You will think of something," he said. "After all, we will not be orphans forever. Someday we will be men, out in the world and on our own."

His words cheered me—as did his friendship. Suddenly I did not feel quite so alone.

Apparently Alonso felt the same way, for he seemed to seek me out whenever possible. We often ate together. And because we were about the same age—and both relatively small—we often worked together. This made the time go by more pleasantly for both of us.

And so the days became weeks and the weeks became months. My memories of life outside the orphanage began to dim.

However, I worked hard at keeping one memory alive—that of my dear mother. Sometimes, after the lights were out, I recited her stories to myself. As long as I could remember them, I reasoned, she was still present in my life. And sometimes, when we had a few minutes to ourselves, I shared her tales with Alonso. He hung on every word. I am sure part of this was because he had never had a mother to tell him stories. At least not that he could recall.

Alonso and I discovered that we thought alike on many things. We both hated Bernardo and loved Doña Rosa. We both liked to be outdoors as much as possible. And, to the despair of the nuns, we both liked to talk.

There was one area, however, where Alonso and I were very different. That was in our feelings about the necessity for lessons. To my surprise, I had discovered that this was my favorite part of each day. The fact that I was a good student seemed equally surprising to Brother

Joseph, the monk who came to the orphanage to teach us.

I loved learning new things. It did not matter what the subject was—mathematics, science, history, geography—I was interested in all of it. But I was especially happy when I quickly mastered the skills of reading and writing. First I learned the alphabet, which I practiced by scratching letters in the dirt. Then I began to put letters together into words. And finally, words became sentences and sentences grew into stories. I was entranced by the idea that stories could be captured somewhere other than in the mind and memory of the storyteller. That they could be written down and handed over to another person—and then to another.

Alonso, however, detested every moment he was forced to spend in the classroom. To his credit, I do not think he was simple, though Brother Joseph often used that word to describe him.

"Spending time at lessons makes no sense to me, Diego," Alonso had once complained to me. "How does all this learning matter, anyway? Books mean nothing to the bees. They do not care how well I read and write. They only care that I know how to keep them content."

One afternoon, Brother Joseph went on and

on at great length about the history of Spain. I found myself caught up in his words, seeing the stories that lay behind the dry facts. Not so for Alonso.

"Can you understand a word of what he is saying?" my friend whispered. "It is all a hopeless muddle to me."

"Do I hear talking?" Brother Joseph asked, lifting his eyes from the pages he had been reading. "During lessons?" His ears were good, for his eyes went directly to the spot where Alonso and I sat side by side.

Brother Joseph got to his feet. This required some effort, as he was extremely fat. He shuffled toward us, his long robes making swishing noises.

I could see beads of sweat gather on Alonso's forehead. He was no favorite of Brother Joseph's. He knew this, and so did I. In fact, the monk had threatened to speak to the nuns about having Alonso expelled from the orphanage if he did not apply himself. If this happened, what would my friend do? Surely he would not survive for long on the streets.

By the time Brother Joseph reached us, Alonso was cowering on the hard bench.

I do not know what made me act. Perhaps it was the look of terror in my friend's eyes.

Whatever the reason, I found myself leaping to my feet.

"I apologize, Brother Joseph," I said. "I was so excited by what you were saying that I forgot myself."

The monk looked at me sternly. "That is understandable, Diego. And your enthusiasm for your studies is commendable. However, you must learn self-control. As a punishment, you will go without dinner tonight."

I nodded and sat down, regretting my foolish gesture. However, as Brother Joseph turned to return to the front of the room, Alonso caught my eye.

His expression told me that I had done the right thing. I only hoped that my empty stomach would understand—and agree.

IV
Betrayed!

As I mentioned earlier, I loved being a student. However, it is fortunate that I am a quick learner, for I had less than a year of schooling. Why? I will explain.

I found myself becoming used to life in the orphanage. As with any life, there were good times and bad. However, I had what I needed—food, shelter, a teacher, and a close friend. So I was not discontented.

Bernardo, however, remained a thorn in my side. I do not know why he especially disliked me. Perhaps because I was so successful in the classroom and he was not. In fact, Brother Joseph once threw up his hands in frustration and exclaimed, "Your head is as thick as the hide of a mule, Bernardo!"

Alonso never minded that he did so poorly in his lessons. But Bernardo did. So that is why I think my studiousness is what made him fix on me as his enemy. And on Alonso as well, although *his* only fault was being my friend.

Whatever the reason, Bernardo did all he could to make our lives miserable. As a result, Alonso and I spent much of our time figuring out where Bernardo might be. And then staying as far away from him as possible.

This was easier than it might have been because neither Alonso nor I did much growing during that year. Bernardo, on the other hand, seemed to become taller and stronger with each passing day. I do not know how he did it on what we were given to eat. I suspect that we were not the only orphans who often lost part of our meals to his greed. Whatever the reason, his size meant that he was assigned to chores that we were not, such as chopping wood for the fires and hauling feed to the cows.

As to the chores, I still hated the chickens. However, thanks to Alonso, I had learned to tolerate the bees. We sometimes worked together to harvest the sticky honey. Of course, I only did what Alonso instructed me to do. He may have been slow in the classroom, but he knew all there was to know about bees.

I preferred chores that required less of my attention. This is why I liked working in the fields. I could think of other things as I weeded, hoed, and picked vegetables. And what I thought about was stories. My head was filled with them—tales my mother had told, the few stories I had read myself, and those Brother Joseph had shared during lessons.

I recited these to myself, adding to them as I pleased. Then I practiced my storytelling skills on the younger children.

"Tell us a tale, Diego," a boy would beg while we worked. Then I would be off, my tongue skipping from word to word like a stone on the surface of a pond. The nuns never complained about this, for the smaller children seemed to work faster as they listened. Before long, it became customary for me to tell stories to the youngest orphans at bedtime as well.

Bernardo, of course, saw this as just one more reason to torment me. "I see you have found your trade, Diego," he sneered one evening as I finished a tale. "You will make a fine nursemaid."

Bernardo's words stung because I knew that one day I would have to leave the safety of the orphanage. I would have to find a way to make a living for myself. The thought was terrifying.

So now, though common sense told me that I should guard my tongue, I did not. "On the contrary, Bernardo," I said. "I shall be able to live by my wits. But what will you do, as you have no wits to fall back upon?"

Bernardo's face turned an interesting shade of purple. His hands clenched into fists and he stepped toward me. I was afraid I had made a fatal mistake.

Fortunately, Sister Dora came by just then. She clapped her hands and cried, "It is bedtime, children." For once, I did not plead for a few more minutes. I hurried to my cot, praying that Bernardo would not seek me out under the cover of darkness and thrash me.

He did not, but his dislike for me turned into something stronger and more serious. I wish now I had not angered him so, for Bernardo took out his anger on Alonso.

It all began when two city officials came to visit. This happened at regular intervals, as there were many permits required to operate the orphanage and its farm. These visits were always an occasion for extra work. Everything inside and out had to be at its best. So for days before, there was little rest. We were always grateful when the officials actually arrived and we could stop working for a few moments.

This visit was no different than any other. The men, both with bald heads, long beards, and large stomachs, arrived at mid-morning. They bowed and exchanged polite greetings with the nuns. Meanwhile, we stood quietly, trying to look properly grateful for the privilege of living in such a fine orphanage. Then the officials went off for refreshments and we were dismissed to go about our usual activities.

By lunchtime, the officials had finished their business and returned to wherever it was they came from. I always wondered why they never stayed to dine with us. I suspect that it was at least partly because our meals were not as fine as what they were used to eating.

Nothing unusual happened until toward the end of our lessons. Late in the afternoon, there was a knock at the classroom door and Sister Teresa entered. Her eyes were cold and her thin face even more stern than usual. She walked to the front of the room and began to talk in hushed tones to Brother Joseph.

"What do you think is going on?" I whispered to Alonso. He merely shrugged. He did not dare answer, since Sister Teresa had turned toward the door and Brother Joseph had turned toward his students.

The monk waited until the door closed behind Sister Teresa. Then he said, "A terrible thing has happened. Terrible. A trust has been violated."

This sounds interesting, I thought.

Brother Joseph began to pace back and forth in front of the room. "This orphanage relies upon the support and approval of Granada's officials," he said. "Yet now that support is threatened."

He whirled, pointed a plump finger at the class, and bellowed, "There is a thief among us! An ungrateful boy who has stolen from one of his betters!"

A murmur ran through the room. "A thief!" whispered Alonso.

"It does not seem possible," I answered, shielding my lips with my hand. I wondered who would be daring enough to do such a thing. And how exactly would he do it? During their visits, the officials stayed as far away from us as possible. They appeared to like the idea of an orphanage—it was the orphans themselves who seemed less than pleasing to them.

There was no chance of Brother Joseph hearing our exchange, I realized. He was still shouting. "This boy shall be found! He shall be punished! The authorities have already been contacted."

The murmurs ceased. This was serious. A boy who was accused and turned over to the authorities would face worse than being expelled from the orphanage. Theft was a serious crime. He would be thrown into prison. And as no one would come to his aid, he would probably rot there. I shuddered, imagining spending the rest of my life locked away in a gray and gloomy cell.

Brother Joseph finished his ranting at last. He dismissed us, saying, "Examine your consciences, my sons. It would be better to confess to your crime than to be found out by others."

It was hard to sort through the rumors that swirled around us for the next twenty-four hours. However, I managed to put together what had happened.

It seemed that one of the officials claimed that his coin purse had been taken. He could have dropped it, he admitted, as the leather thong that held it had come untied. But upon finding such a treasure, an honest orphan would have seen that it was returned to its rightful owner. Since it was not, whoever had found it must be a thief.

From the kitchen to the dormitory to the chicken house, every corner of the orphanage was searched. We, of course, did the searching. But we were always under the supervision of one of the nuns as we did so.

Finally it was bedtime on the day after the officials' visit. The night before, with all the searching, there had been no opportunity for me to tell a story to the small children. However, tonight they begged for one.

"Please, Sister Dora," pleaded a small, pale boy. "May Diego tell us a tale before it is time for bed?"

"Very well," the old nun said. "As long as it is a short one, Diego."

I nodded and gathered the little ones around me. I began to tell them one of my favorites—a tale of knighthood in which the hero was known as El Cid. The story was a true one, and one I had first heard from my mother.

As I spoke, I noted that Alonso sat on the end of his bunk, listening. The story of El Cid was one of his favorites as well, so I was not surprised.

What did surprise me was that Bernardo stood nearby. Other than mocking me as a nurse-maid, he paid little attention to my stories. I wondered why he was listening so intently now.

Then, just as I reached the part of the story where El Cid kneels to pledge his loyalty to the new king, Bernardo gasped.

We all turned to look at him. He was staring at Alonso's cot. "What is it, Bernardo?" asked Sister Dora, somewhat impatiently. (She had been listening to my story as well.)

"Look, Sister," responded Bernardo. He pointed to the thin mattress. "There is something under Alonso's mattress."

"Well, let us see what it is so Diego can

continue," said the Sister.

Bernardo gave me a strange smile. Meanwhile, Alonso got to his feet and lifted the corner of the mattress.

"The missing coin purse!" shouted Bernardo. "Alonso, you are a thief! Sister, come and look."

"I-I-I am not a thief!" protested Alonso, who had made no move to pick up the leather purse.

It was Sister Dora who removed the purse from its hiding place. Her face was white as she looked at Alonso. "I never would have expected this of you," she said.

"I did not do it!" Alonso cried.

By now, of course, I was on my feet. "Alonso is as honest as the day is long, Sister," I said. "You know this to be true."

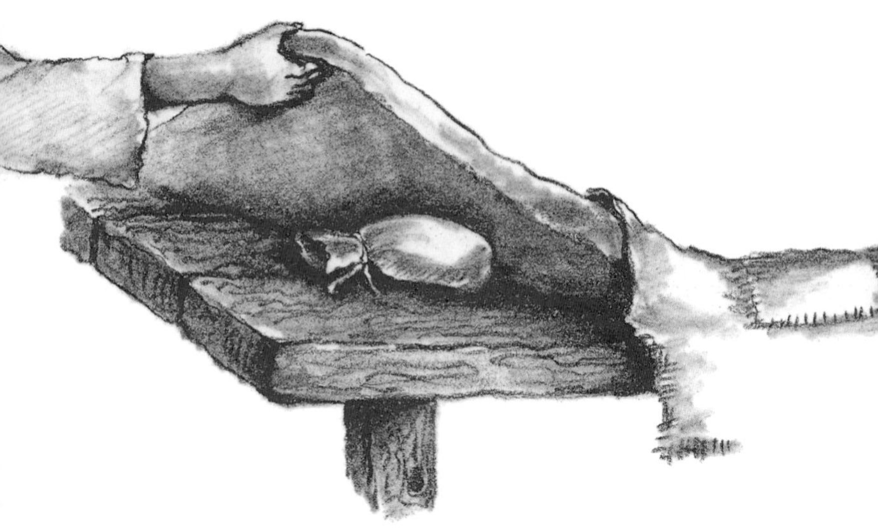

"Then why is the purse hidden under his mattress?" asked Bernardo. His face bore a look of unusual virtue, as if he had never had an evil thought or done an evil deed.

"Why indeed?" I returned. "The dormitory has already been searched. So how did it get here, Bernardo? Perhaps you know something about the matter?"

Bernardo made as if to attack me, but Sister Dora's voice held him back. "Into your beds! All of you!" she ordered.

Then she turned to Alonso. "You must come with me, Alonso," she said. "Perhaps you can explain yourself to Sister Teresa."

Sister Dora did not seem to be any happier than I was. In fact, the only person in the room who was smiling was Bernardo.

I watched helplessly as Alonso left the room, herded forward by Sister Dora.

The Escape

Alonso did not return that night. I lay on my cot, unable to sleep. All I could think of was the frightened look my friend had given me as he left the room.

The dormitory was silent except for the soft breathing of my fellow orphans. Even Bernardo is asleep, I thought bitterly. And why not? He has no conscience to keep him awake.

I *knew* Bernardo was behind Alonso's troubles. He must have found—or even stolen—the coin purse. Then he had planted it under my friend's mattress.

I did wonder why he had picked Alonso to label as a thief, and not me. Perhaps he had been unable to get to my cot. Certainly he knew that hurting Alonso would also hurt me. So it probably mattered little to him which one of us was accused.

I could no longer lie there doing nothing.

I carefully pushed my ragged blanket to one side. Then, without a sound, I swung my legs over the side of the cot. I sat up, then waited—listening for any response to my movement.

No one stirred. Carrying my shoes, I tiptoed past the sleeping boys. I worried about opening the heavy wooden door. Would it creak noisily and give me away?

The fates were with me, for the door opened without a sound. Still on tiptoe, I made my way down the long stairs. The only light came from a lantern that burned in the entry hall below. But I needed little light. I had been going up and down these stairs for almost a year. I knew every inch of every step.

At the bottom, I paused to slip on my soft-soled shoes—and to think. I needed a plan. A plan of escape. For that was what I had decided Alonso and I had to do. But first I had to find my friend—provided he was still within the orphanage walls.

I felt he must be. Surely the nuns had not turned him over to the authorities yet. They were fond of Alonso. They would at least wait until morning, when Brother Joseph arrived. After all, *he* was the one who had threatened to bring in the authorities. They would be reluctant to carry out such a threat on their own.

But where could Alonso be now? I wondered. In a spot where someone could keep an eye on him, I was sure.

Then I knew where I would find him. The infirmary! That was one place that was open no matter how late the hour. Someone was always on hand in case a boy became ill during the night. Sister Ursula would be on duty tonight, as she always was.

My spirits lifted slightly. Sister Ursula was hardly the best guardian in all of Granada. I myself had found her sound asleep at her post one night when I had a toothache. I had been forced to raise my voice and shake her gently to wake her.

I continued on my way through the quiet halls. The infirmary lay behind the kitchen, at the back of the building.

A lantern cast its shadowed glow out into the hall. I stood beside the door, out of sight, and listened. The only sound was that of soft snores. As I had suspected, Sister Ursula was sound asleep.

I took a deep breath and slipped inside. The good sister was slumped to one side on a straight-backed chair. Her mouth hung open slightly and her chin quivered with each breath.

At the other side of the room, on a cot under the window, lay Alonso. I edged toward him, creeping along at an angle to keep one eye on Sister Ursula.

I reached the cot without alerting her. At the same time, I placed one hand over Alonso's mouth and used the other to shake him awake.

He opened his eyes at once. They were filled with fear, but rapidly turned to recognition and then to hope. Releasing him, I warned him to be silent by putting one finger to my lips. He nodded, then sat up. I motioned toward the door and he nodded again. I pointed at his shoes. A third nod and he picked them up.

Then we tiptoed out of the room. I had a momentary concern for Sister Ursula, who would be criticized severely for letting Alonso escape. But my greater concern was for my friend. Life in prison would be far worse for him than a few moments of unpleasantness would be for Sister Ursula.

Together we entered the kitchen, which at this hour was quiet and empty. Another moment and we were outside, walking past Doña Rosa's herb garden. Five minutes after that, we were in the fields, picking our way carefully by the light of the moon. And ten minutes later, we had arrived at the edge of the river. Not until then did Alonso speak.

"Diego, wait!" he said. "Where are we going?"

"We are leaving the orphanage," I said.

"Leaving? We cannot leave."

"We have no choice, Alonso," I explained patiently. "If we stay, you will go to prison."

"But I did not steal anything," he said. "You *must* believe me!"

"Of course I do," I assured him. "I am sure that Bernardo is behind the whole thing. I am equally sure that we will never be able to prove it. And that Brother Joseph will see you go to prison, if for no other reason than to quiet the complaints of the official whose coin purse was taken."

My words sobered Alonso. He knew I spoke the truth. Bernardo was both evil and clever. There was no way we would ever be able to beat him.

"You are right," said Alonso in a mournful voice. "I have to go. Even though it means that I may never become a beekeeper. But you should stay here, Diego. You have told me many times that you are not eager to go out into the world when the time comes that you must. Certainly you do not want to do so now, before you are forced to."

"I will not stay here without you," I said firmly. "I could not stand it. To have Bernardo look at me every day, gloating over your leaving.

And rejoicing that he was able to hurt me by doing harm to you. No, my friend, we will go together.

"Besides," I continued, "we will have a better chance together than apart. We are going to live by our wits. And, as Brother Joseph always says, 'Two sets of wits are far better than one.' "

I had convinced Alonso. So we began to follow the rough path that led along the riverbank. As I mentioned before, the orphanage grounds were fenced, but it was easy to get past the fence where it met the river. We merely swung ourselves around the last post and we were on the other side.

I am not sure I remember exactly how I felt about our sudden freedom. I know there was a certain amount of fear on my part. But there was excitement as well. In a matter of two years or so, we would be old enough to be out on our own, after all. The next phase of our lives was merely beginning a bit earlier than anticipated. *If* we could manage not to be caught.

"Leaving the orphanage is not enough, Alonso," I said. "We must leave Granada."

"What? Why must we?"

"Because the authorities will be looking for you," I explained.

My friend nodded his head sadly. "Then we should leave, I suppose," he said. "Where shall we go?"

"Seville," I replied. I do not know what made that destination pop into my head. I had never been out of Granada, and I knew almost nothing about Seville. However, the city was far enough away and large enough that I was sure we would not be found.

We walked the rest of that night, putting Granada behind us forever. We kept to the edge of the road, where we could take cover if another traveler came along.

I knew that Seville was due west, then slightly to the north. However, I did not know enough about the stars to use them as a guide. So I was grateful when the sun finally began to peek above the horizon and warm our backs. We could use it as a compass.

Later that morning, we heard someone coming along behind us. "Come, Alonso," I said, "we must get out of sight."

We ducked into a patch of reeds. It was swampy, but wet feet were far better than being captured.

It was a caravan of gypsies. I knew we had nothing to fear from them, so I signaled to Alonso and we stepped out into the road.

"What have we here?" asked a tall man. He wore several earrings and had a colorful cloth wrapped around his brow.

"We are travelers, sir," I said politely.

"As are we," said the gypsy.

"May we join you then?"

The man nodded and we fell in with the caravan. The gypsies were friendly, but showed no curiosity about us. Still, I soon found myself explaining that we had recently escaped from an orphanage.

"And well that you did," said an elderly woman. "No one should be locked up in such a place. Not when there is a whole great world to roam."

And so we were adopted by the group. They were generous, offering to share their food and inviting us to stay with them if we wanted. They, too, were headed west, their leader explained, though not as far as Seville. They would veer to the south before reaching the city. "You are welcome to join us," he added, "for as long as you care to."

That suited us just fine for the time being. The gypsies are wanderers. They carry all their belongings in their covered wagons. Their journeys take them wherever they want to go. If they like an area, they stay there as long as the weather is good, or until they feel the urge to move again, or until the animals need more land for grazing.

So even if this band of gypsies was not going all the way to Seville, they would be company for part of the journey. And we would not have to sleep out in the open by ourselves.

That evening, we sat around the campfire with our traveling companions. As the flames soared into the sky, several gypsies began singing. Others clapped their hands and stomped their feet in time to the music.

"Are you celebrating a special occasion?" I inquired.

"We do not need a reason to celebrate," answered a young woman.

"That is right," said another. She laughed and added, "All a gypsy needs to be happy is a voice to sing, hands to clap, and feet fit to dance."

Alonso and I were caught up in the excitement as well. We clapped our hands and stomped our feet as if we, too, had gypsy blood running through our veins.

We traveled with the gypsies for several days more. It might have been faster to go on our own, but we had no reason to get to Seville quickly.

At last we reached the spot where our paths

diverged. “You are welcome to come along with us,” the leader said.

It was tempting to accept the invitation. However, something pulled us toward Seville. We conferred for a few moments, then announced our decision to follow our original plan. Our reasoning was that we had escaped the orphanage to be on our own. We were not about to give up the new-found freedom we had gained. So we said good-bye and struck out to the northwest—to Seville.

VI

Seville

By the time we arrived in Seville, we were tired, thirsty, and hungry. For the last 24 hours of our journey, all we had eaten was some fruit the workers in an orange grove had given us. Nothing had ever tasted sweeter! However, our stomachs had hardly been satisfied.

Now all our troubles were forgotten in the excitement of having safely reached our destination. Seville was all that I had imagined. Besides being Spain's richest and most populated city, it is beautiful. At this time of year—early autumn—it was still filled with flowers.

We wandered around for most of the day. We spent some time in the port area of the city. Seville is located on a river. This river is deep enough and wide enough for seafaring vessels. And because it is far from the coast, it is safe from the pirates who ravage the open seas.

A fleet of ships was being readied for a trip to the Indies, so the port was bustling with activity.

Heavily loaded barges sailed up and down the river. Dozens of great ships lay at anchor, their masts towering over the port. Mountains of cargo were piled up on the riverbank, waiting to be transported to the New World. We walked about, staring in awe at the wondrous sights.

By late afternoon, we had left the port and wandered into an area of inns and cafes. The smell of food made me remember that we had eaten nothing all day.

"Perhaps someone will be willing to share a scrap of food in exchange for our services," I suggested to Alonso.

We loitered near the outdoor tables of a cafe. For a time, we made ourselves useful by picking up fallen objects, fetching drinks, and doing other small tasks. To our satisfaction, several men tossed us coins for our efforts. These we immediately converted into food for ourselves. Then we sat down to eat.

Conversation swirled around us. I realized that many of our fellow diners were experienced sailors who were getting ready for other journeys to the Indies. They spoke of the ships they had sailed on in the past as well as those they planned to sail on soon. They boasted of treasures they hoped to find and those that had already been brought back to Spain.

I was very interested in what these men had to say. I had learned something of Spain's voyages of discovery from Brother Joseph. Almost 50 years had passed since Christopher Columbus' first journey to the Indies, which he had claimed for Spain. Still, the excitement had not faded. Twice each year, in the spring and fall, a fleet of Spanish ships sailed to the New World. Months later, it returned with every ship's hold stuffed full of treasure.

I knew that at this very moment Spaniards were conquering and settling the lands of the New World. They gave these lands names such as New Spain and Golden Castile—names that reminded them of home.

The men talked of more than their journeys. They also described many of the wonders they had seen. Houses made of branches and sticks instead of clay tiles. A bed called a *hamaca,* which was like a net hung above the floor. Foods with strange names like *guava, avocado,* and *tomato.* Their stories satisfied my spirit in the same way that the food satisfied my stomach.

"What is this tower they speak of?" asked Alonso. He had been paying more attention to his food than to the talk that went on around us.

"The Tower of Gold," I explained. "Brother

Joseph told us about it, Alonso. It is the king's treasury. Goods from the Indies are stored there when they first arrive. You know from our lessons that Spain's monarch receives one-fifth of all the treasures brought back from the New World. The Tower of Gold is where the king's share is kept until it is presented to him."

Alonso nodded, then went back to his bread and fruit. I leaned forward to listen more intently. A bearded man at the next table noticed me. "What have we here?" he said. "An eavesdropper?"

My cheeks burned with embarrassment. "I apologize, sir," I murmured. "It is just that your stories are so interesting."

The man laughed. "Yes, they are, boy. The Indies is a fascinating place."

"Please, sir," I said, "did your ship bring back any treasure?"

"Aye, lad, we did. Silver—and pearls as well."

I went on to ask question after question. The gentleman did not seem to mind my attention. To be truthful, he seemed flattered, and his stories grew more and more dramatic.

By the time he finished, it was dark. Alonso was half asleep at the table. I shook him by the shoulder.

"Wh-wh-what is it?" he stammered.

"We must go, Alonso," I said.

"Go where?" he asked.

It was a good question. We had nowhere to go. However, we had passed a large stone bridge that spanned the river. It was not far from where we sat, and it would offer us some shelter until morning.

"Follow me," I said.

Not long afterward, we huddled together under the bridge, hidden from sight by one of its massive stone supports. The great structure was old—built by the Romans long ago, when they controlled Spain and most of Europe. The fact that it was still standing now, more than a thousand years later, made it seem a haven from danger.

The only lights to be seen were the pinpricks of lanterns that lined the marketplace in the distance. But soon even those had been doused.

Fortunately it was a warm night, so we did not miss our thin blankets. However, I would have been grateful for even the poor mattress that had been mine at the orphanage.

To take our minds off the hard ground and the dark that pressed down upon us, I began to tell a story. It was about a brave adventurer who set sail for the Indies.

I must have fallen asleep before finishing, for I have no memory of how the tale ended. I do remember that I dreamed of the Indies that night.

Two weeks later, Alonso and I were still spending our nights under the same bridge. We were not alone, of course. The morning after our first night in Seville, we had discovered that other unfortunates with no place to lay their heads shared the space with us. However, they did not bother us, and we did not bother them.

The authorities concerned us more than our fellow residents did. There was always the danger of being picked up as vagrants—poor souls with no means of support and no homes. Then we would be taken off to another orphanage, or perhaps even to prison. Neither of those options appealed to us. So we took care not to leave behind any signs that we were sleeping under the bridge. Everything we owned we either carried with us or hid during the day. Fortunately, we owned very little.

We spent the daylight hours wandering Seville. Within a week, we knew the city like the backs of our hands.

"Shall we go to the market today?" I asked Alonso one morning.

"Why not?" he shrugged.

The public market was a bustling place. People went there to shop for the food they would eat that day, to meet friends, to chat, and to hear the latest news and gossip. Alonso and I could usually find some work there. We would help men unload their carts, carry heavy pots and pans for the cooks, or deliver bundles of goods to those who had purchased them.

By now, we were familiar faces in the plaza. The shopkeepers knew us, and knew that we were honest. We had pledged that we would never sink so low as to steal in order to eat. So far we had been lucky. Our stomachs stayed full enough to allow us to keep that promise.

Still, running errands would not support us forever. We needed to find a better way to live. I studied the market square today with that thought in mind.

"Look over there, Alonso," I said.

"Where?"

"At that juggler," I said, pointing to one corner of the plaza. A sizable crowd had gathered to watch and listen as a colorfully dressed man tossed oranges into the air. But what really drew my attention was that some of the spectators were dropping coins into a little box the entertainer had placed before him on the ground.

"We could do that," I noted.

"I am not so sure," said Alonso. "Have you ever tried juggling?"

"No," I admitted. "But how hard could it be?"

We moved closer, pushing our way through the crowd to get near the front. The man was now juggling three balls made of a shiny fabric. The bright colors gleamed in the sun as the balls danced in the air.

The entertainer went on to juggle bottles, peacock feathers, and other objects large and small. At last he paused. The crowd began to move away, but Alonso and I stood there.

"Please, sir, can you show me how you do that?" I asked.

He looked me over slowly, taking in my ragged clothes and muddy shoes. For a moment, I thought he was going to ignore my request. But then he nodded and said, "Watch."

I did so for five minutes. At the end of that time, the juggler asked, "Would you like to try it yourself?"

"Yes," I said eagerly.

He handed me three balls. I tossed all three into the air at once. All three fell immediately to the ground. Behind me, I heard someone laugh. I hoped it was only Alonso.

"No," said the juggler. "The technique is really quite simple. Throw the balls one at a time and keep your head still. Do not try to follow the arc of the first ball with your eyes."

I tried again. It sounded simple, but it was not.

After my third attempt, I picked up the three balls and handed them back to the juggler. I would not be making my living this way, it was clear.

We moved on. Close by, a storyteller was just winding down a tale. His audience clapped, then began to drift off. However, many of them first dropped coins into the box at the man's feet.

"That is it!" I said to Alonso.

"What is it?"

"We can become storytellers!" I announced. After all, I reasoned, I loved to tell stories. And the small children at the orphanage had been mesmerized when I shared my tales with them.

Dragging Alonso by one arm, I headed for an empty spot near the edge of the square. I took up a position there.

"Put out your hat for donations," I ordered.

Alonso shrugged, then took off his hat and held it stiffly in front of him.

I launched into my favorite story—the one about El Cid. No one stopped to listen. They all walked right on by, intent on their business or their conversations. A few glanced in my direction, then quickly looked the other way.

"I am not tall enough," I said in despair.

"I fear you are not clean enough," said my friend.

Alonso might have a point, I realized. I was not convinced that the performers were actually much cleaner than I was. However, they wore costumes that were as entertaining as their acts were. Costumes that drew the attention of audiences in a positive way. In short, they were pleasant to look at. After weeks on the road and under a bridge, I was not.

"Come on, Diego," Alonso said. "I am hungry. If we do not earn a few coins this morning, I shall stay hungry." He returned his cap to his head and stalked off. I had no choice but to follow. I was hungry as well.

We spent the rest of the morning moving around. This was important, as staying in one place too long could attract the attention of the authorities. By midday, we had done several errands and earned enough to buy some bread and a small hunk of cheese. We took our food to a quiet corner and sat there to eat, our backs against the stone wall.

"I would like to go back to the port this afternoon," I said as soon as I had swallowed the last bite.

"Why?"

"I want to see if any more ships have arrived to join the fleet that is leaving soon for the Indies," I said.

"That is all you think of," muttered Alonso. "What good does the New World do us, I ask you?"

"What harm does it do?" I returned.

"It puts ideas into your head. Ideas that can never happen."

I stared at my friend in surprise. It was the first time that Alonso had ever objected to visiting the port area. Usually he was as eager to do so as I was.

"What is the matter with you?" I asked.

"I am sick of this," he admitted. "Sick of sleeping under a bridge. Sick of wondering if I will have anything to eat. Sick of worrying about what is to become of us. And sorry that you have been forced to live this way because of me."

"I was not forced," I protested. "It was my idea to come to Seville. And I am glad we did."

I was at a loss as to what was bothering my

friend. After all, he was not in prison, where he could have been.

I, on the other hand, was perfectly happy. True, while living in the orphanage, I had expressed some concern about having to leave when I was older. But now that we were on our own, I, for the most part, was glad of it. Now I asked, "What would you have us do, then?"

Alonso shook his head. "I don't know, Diego. Forget I said anything. We will go to the port."

And so we did. A huge ship had arrived only the day before. It was now being loaded with cargo for its long journey to the New World. Barrels and crates were lifted off carts and carried onto the ship. The cargo would provide huge profits for the merchants and investors who were funding the journey.

We stayed for several hours, watching and listening. Reluctantly, as the light began to fade, I followed Alonso back to our home under the bridge. There we ate a meager meal of stale bread and settled down for the night.

I was awake long after Alonso had fallen asleep. My friend was right—a visit to the port *did* fill my head with ideas. I saw myself on the deck of a great ship that was headed downriver, toward the sea. If only I could set sail for the New

World. I would make my fortune, I was sure of it. And what stories I would have to tell upon my return!

It must have been long after midnight when I finally drifted into slumber, for the sun was high in the sky by the time I woke. I rolled over, groaning when my elbow hit a rock. Then, rubbing my eyes, I sat up.

Alonso was gone!

On My Own

I sat there for over an hour, sure that my friend would return. That he had just tired of waiting for me to wake up and had gone in search of breakfast.

However, he did not appear. At last I got up and walked slowly toward the marketplace. Along the way, I looked in every spot where Alonso could possibly be. There was no sign of him.

By the time I reached the marketplace, I was hungry. I headed for the shop of Don Eduardo, the baker who had given us bread the day before. His shop was very small, and he worked there alone. He often let us take leftover goods in return for sweeping the floor or carrying piles of wood for the oven.

"Good morning, Diego," Don Eduardo greeted me. "Where is your friend?"

"I do not know," I admitted. "Have you seen him this morning?"

Don Eduardo shook his head. "No, but I have been busy. I have not had a moment to poke my head outside the bakery."

I spent several minutes helping Don Eduardo. He told me to come back at the end of the day and he would give me something to eat. Then I left, intent on finding Alonso.

First I made the rounds of the marketplace, talking to all the shopkeepers I knew. None of them had seen my friend since the day before.

Then I walked all around the city, looking everywhere we had been since our arrival. I saw no trace of Alonso. It was as if he had vanished.

Late that afternoon, I headed back to the marketplace. I did not know what to do next or where else to look. Head down, I entered Don Eduardo's bakery.

"Ah, Diego," he said, "I have been watching for you."

"Why? Have you seen Alonso?"

The baker dusted his floury hands on his apron and motioned for me to sit. "I have heard something," he began. His round face expressed concern.

"About Alonso?"

"Yes. One of the fruit vendors told me he had seen him this morning. He said that Alonso ran up and snatched a melon—in plain sight of a policeman who was standing there."

"What?" I cried, jumping to my feet. "He would never do such a thing!"

"That is what the man saw. He said it was as if Alonso *wanted* to be caught."

"Where is he now?" I asked. Visions of my friend in a prison cell filled my mind. This was what we had run away to avoid!

"The policeman said something about the orphanage," Don Eduardo replied. "The fruit vendor heard him ask Alonso where he lived and how old he was. Alonso said that he had no home and that he was nine years old."

My friend had taken advantage of his small size and shaved a few years off his age. He knew that being younger would increase his chances of being taken to an orphanage rather than to prison. He probably *had* wanted to be caught, I realized.

"Do you know which orphanage?" I asked.

Don Eduardo shook his head. "No. And unless you want to end up there yourself, I suggest that you do not go in search of it," he said.

He looked at me intently before going on. "I am not a man who asks many questions, Diego. Therefore I do not know where you came from before you arrived here. However, I suspect that you do not want to go back to wherever it is. So I am concerned for you. You are too young to be on your own in a city like this for long."

Though I was not as young as Don Eduardo might suspect, I knew he was right. But what was I to do about the matter?

I thanked the baker for his news and for the bread that he offered me. Then I bid him good-bye.

"Come and see me tomorrow," he called as I left the shop. "I will have some more bread for you, I am sure. And, Diego—think about what I said."

I nodded and trudged off, not sure where I was going. I was afraid to return to my home under the bridge. What if the policeman had made Alonso show him where he had been living? I might walk into a trap. Even if Alonso wanted to return to the security of the orphanage, I did not.

As I walked, I chewed on a crust of bread. I also considered and discarded several plans for finding and rescuing Alonso. I knew there was nothing I could do. Besides, I was not sure that my friend *wanted* to be rescued. I could only hope that he was truly not in a prison cell somewhere, but in an orphanage.

He may be happier this way, I thought. Perhaps he will once again be able to work with the bees, as he so loves to do.

By now it was dark and the air was becoming chilly. I shivered in my thin clothing, thinking about the night ahead. At last I took shelter under a bush that grew close to the wall of a stone building. It offered some protection from the nighttime breeze. I don't think I actually slept, but at least I was not out wandering in the night.

Before dawn the next morning, I set off again. Without really thinking about it, my feet took me straight to the port. The sun was rising as I approached. It lit the masts of the great ships that were tied up at the wharf. Gulls circled about overhead, filling the air with their screechy cries. The water lapped up against the docks, a sound that was both soothing and restless.

I tipped my head back to look at the top of one great mast. The flag of Spain hung there, fluttering in the gentle wind.

Suddenly I knew what I had to do. No more dreaming of a voyage to the New World. It was time to go! I would sign on as a crew member on one of the sailing ships. It was almost the end of September, and the fleet would be leaving soon. I had only to find a captain who was willing to accept my services. In a matter of days, I would be on the high seas, headed for a new life in a new world.

I walked toward the slanted walkway that led from the wharf to the deck of the ship.

VIII

I Remain Landlocked

As I finished talking, the sailor's laughter boomed out over the water. Several men on the deck stopped their work and looked up.

My heart plummeted. This sailor's reaction was similar to what I had experienced on other ships. When he quieted, I said, "Please, sir. I *do* want to join your crew. If you would be kind enough to take me to your captain."

"That I will not do, boy," the sailor said. "The captain would have my head for wasting his time with the likes of you."

"Why?" I protested. "I am honest. I am not afraid of hard work. And I know how to read and write."

"All fine qualities," he said. "But skills like reading and writing are not what we need on the high seas."

"Then what necessary skills do I lack?" I inquired mournfully. I already knew what I would hear—I had heard it before. Still, I had to ask.

The sailor looked at my face, then said, "I am sorry I laughed, lad. I see that you are serious. However, you lack everything that is necessary. Years, for one thing. You are too young."

"I am older than I look," I said.

"Well, then, how much experience do you have as a seaman?" he asked.

I shrugged. "None," I admitted. "But I am a fast learner."

"Do you have anything else to offer? Do you know navigation? Have you a trade that would be useful on the voyage, such as sail-making or carpentry? Or do you have money to pay for your passage instead?"

I had to answer no to all of his questions. I had absolutely nothing of importance to offer any captain or crew.

"Then you had best be on your way," the sailor said, not unkindly. "You can travel to the New World when you are older and know more about the sea."

For a moment, thoughts of stowing away flashed through my mind. I had heard stories of men who had done so, hiding aboard a ship before it sailed. But they did not dare be seen during the voyage, so most times they died before reaching their destination. No wonder, hiding in a barrel or crate with no food or water for five weeks or more! So I did not consider the idea for long.

Instead, I left the deck. I walked much more slowly than I had when coming aboard. I would not be traveling to the New World on this ship.

Or, apparently, on any other. It appeared that my dream of a new life was only that—a dream.

The next few days passed in a blur. I missed Alonso's companionship terribly. While it had seemed an adventure to be in Seville together, it was frightening and lonely without him.

During the day, I wandered from the marketplace to the wharves. At night, I slept wherever I could find shelter. I kept myself company in the dark by reciting stories out loud. The sound of my own voice made me forget for a time that I was alone. And the stories themselves provided some comfort.

By the end of the week, I had come to the realization that I needed a real job. Something that would provide me with a regular income so I could afford lodging. Of course, I was qualified to do nothing to earn such an income. So it appeared that I would have to learn a trade.

I approached Don Eduardo first, as he had been kind to me. "Would you take me on as your apprentice?" I asked the baker. "I have had some experience with making bread."

"I wish I could, Diego," he said, "but my business is not big enough to support myself, my family, and an apprentice."

Then he looked thoughtful. "However, there is another bakery in the square. Surely you have passed it?"

I had. Don Manuel Mercado, the owner of that bakery, had been far less generous than Don Eduardo. So Alonso and I had spent little time in Don Manuel's shop.

"I have heard that his apprentice was taken ill and that he is going back to his family. And that Don Manuel is looking for a new apprentice," Don Eduardo said. "I will speak to him about you."

So that is how I found myself standing in front of Don Manuel in his large shop. The baker looked me up and down critically.

"I am not in the habit of taking on boys who do not come from decent families," he said. "However, Don Eduardo assures me that you are honest. So you will be my apprentice on a trial basis. You will serve for seven years. In return for your services, I will provide you with room and board, but no pay. Is that understood?"

I nodded, grateful to know that I would have a place to sleep and food to eat. And while I had never entertained thoughts of being a baker, the opportunity to learn any trade was a valuable one. If I did well enough, I might someday be a master baker, as Don Manuel and

Don Eduardo were.

My new master and his wife lived on the second floor of the building that housed the bakery. I was not to live there, however. Instead, I was given a small room downstairs, at the back. I had a bed with a mattress and bedcovers, a chair, and a washbasin. I had not slept in a real bed since my days in the orphanage!

Much of the rest of the first floor was taken up with the supplies and tools used in baking. There were huge bags of flour, buckets, kneading troughs, pots and pans, heating stones, and work tables. The shop itself was at the front of the building. That is where customers came to place and pick up their orders.

The baker's wife, Doña Elena, was a fine woman. She was short and plump and always cheerful. You would never see her idle. She was either cooking or spinning or sewing or cleaning. And after doing all her chores upstairs, she would come downstairs to see if there was anything she could do to help in the bakery. From the first day, she seemed fond of me, perhaps because she had no son of her own. She sometimes slipped me a little something extra to eat. And occasionally, as we worked side by side, she told me stories or listened to mine.

The duties of a baker's apprentice were many.

One of the most important was to take care of the oven. As with most ovens, it was made of mud and shaped like a beehive. (Actually, it made me think of Alonso and his love of beekeeping.) I had to keep the oven well-supplied with dry firewood, stacking the wood just so at the back to ensure an even temperature for baking. I also had to check regularly to see if any cracks formed on the outside of the oven. If they did, it was my job to seal them with more mud. Otherwise, air would get inside and the temperature would fall.

In addition to these chores, I had to constantly clean the oven, raking out the embers and sweeping ashes from the bottom. And, of course, I had to be sure to remove the loaves of bread at the right time.

Month followed month, and things were going well. I worked without complaint from the time I woke until the time I went to bed. I quickly learned how to keep the oven at exactly the temperature it should be. I kept the woodpile stacked high and swept the floors until the clouds of flour made me sneeze.

After some time, my master occasionally entrusted me with the duty of mixing the bread dough. I liked the feeling of the dough in my hands. When mixed properly, it seemed almost alive.

Although Don Manuel usually spoke to me only to give orders, Doña Elena often paid me compliments. "You have a good head on your shoulders, Diego," she said one day. "You will make a fine baker."

However, it was not to be. As time went by, boredom began to set in. After all, baking one loaf of bread is much like baking another. By the end of the first eight months of my apprenticeship, I knew for certain that I was much fonder of eating bread than of making it.

That was also when my master began to voice serious complaints about my work. I admit that he had some grounds to do so. Once I was daydreaming and neglected to notice that a beggar had entered the shop. He grabbed a loaf of fresh bread and ran off. (I paid for that mistake by going without dinner for several nights!) Once I was so busy listening to a customer's tale of a trip to Toledo that I gave him the wrong change. (Another night with nothing to eat!) And several times I had to be reminded to gather a load of kindling to start the fire the next morning. There may have been other instances, but if so, I have forgotten them.

Each time I was scolded, I promised to try harder to keep my mind on my work. I always meant what I said, and I truly did try.

Then came the day that my master had to visit the miller to talk business. Before Don Manuel left, he said, "Diego, you are in charge of the shop while I am gone. Do not forget that you must watch the loaves that are in the oven now."

I nodded. Of course I would watch them. I would take them out at exactly the right moment, when they were brown, crusty, and fully baked.

Unfortunately, I was distracted. I went out to the street to dump a bucket of dirty water. A small crowd had gathered nearby, listening to a storyteller.

I did not often get to the plaza now, as my duties kept me busy. So the temptation was strong. I decided to listen for just a few minutes. Perhaps I would learn a new tale to recite to Doña Elena.

The entertainer's story was not new. Instead, it was one that was very familiar to me. As I listened, I found myself remembering when I had last heard the tale—

"Tell it again, Mama," I begged. "Please."

"Very well, Diego," she said, pulling me closer to her. We sat side by side in front of the fire in our small home.

"Once upon a time there was a land of great abundance," she began. "All the beasts lived

happily, except for one thing. There was a fierce lion who threatened to eat them. So one day the animals gathered together to discuss their problem. They decided to go to talk to the lion . . ."

I could feel my mother's arms around me. I could hear her gentle voice.

Suddenly I came back to the present. It was the storyteller's voice I heard, not my mother's. And it was my master's angry face I saw, not her loving gaze. Don Manuel was walking down the street—and he had seen me standing in the square and listening.

I dashed back to the oven, but it was too late to avoid disaster. Smoke was billowing in great dark clouds. The eight loaves inside the oven looked more like lumps of charcoal than crusty bread.

"You are hopeless!" thundered Don Manuel. "I would be better off with no apprentice than I am with you! It is *my* good name you are ruining. When I tell a customer his bread will be ready at a certain time, I mean it. But you have made that impossible."

I hung my head, listening to him rant for a while longer. His wife tried to intervene, saying that I was only a boy. But my master would not budge.

"He has his head in the clouds," he said. "He cannot keep his mind on his work. If he stays, we will soon be out of business!"

He was exaggerating, of course. However, we would never find out.

"Your apprenticeship is over, Diego," Don Manuel announced. His expression made it clear that there was no point in asking for another chance.

In a matter of moments, I had gathered together my few belongings and left the bakery for the last time. Once again, I was on my own with no means of support and nowhere to go.

IX

Stables and Stories

I found myself dividing my time between the port and the marketplace. By now, I was a familiar sight in both places. After all, I had been in Seville for more than a full year. By my reckoning, I would be 12 years old in a matter of months. However, I still looked younger.

Seville never gets particularly cold, but as fall approached, the nights became chilly. I missed my bed at the back of the bakery. I also missed cheerful Doña Elena. I did not miss her gruff husband at all.

As the nights grew cooler, someone took pity on me. It was Benito, a servant in one of the fine houses near the marketplace. We had become friends of a sort, often finding opportunities to talk while he ran errands for his master.

"You look like you have not slept in days,

Diego," he said to me one morning when we met outside a shop.

I shrugged. "It is hard to sleep when one is shivering all night long," I admitted.

Benito glanced at the shop to be sure no one was paying attention to us. Then he leaned closer and spoke in a low, hurried voice. "Come to the stable tonight after dark. The groom is a friend of mine. I will see to it that he lets you take shelter there."

"Thank you," I murmured. Then Benito hurried off to finish his errands.

That night I made my way to the narrow alley behind the grand house where Benito worked. I knew that I would find the stables there. As I approached, I heard a whispered voice. "Who is there?"

"It is I, Diego," I said. I could not see anyone in the dark. I had to trust that the speaker was Benito's friend. Otherwise, I might be running through the streets to avoid being captured by the angry homeowner.

"Come this way," the voice said. A figure stepped out of the shadows and motioned to me to follow.

He led me to a stall at the rear of the stable. To my relief, I was to be the stall's only occupant for the night. I murmured my thanks and sank down onto the scratchy straw. It was a pleasure to be under a roof and out of the wind.

I lay there, listening to the huffing of breath and the shuffling of hooves. These sounds were far more comforting than the rustlings I heard in the straw. I knew that mice and snakes liked to live in stables. I could only hope that they were as eager to avoid me as I was to avoid them.

Still, I was too tired to worry long about any bedfellows I might have. I fell into a deep sleep that lasted until early the next morning. It might have lasted longer if I had not been awakened.

"Up!" whispered an urgent voice. "You must get up now!"

I opened my eyes and found myself face-to-face with a worried young man. He sported a thin mustache and a straggly beard. His hair was curly and uncombed.

"Are you Benito's friend?" I asked as I got to my feet.

"Yes," he replied. "My name is Pedro and I am the groom here."

Now that I was on my feet, Pedro seemed more relaxed. "Come," he said, "I will show you around. Just be ready to run for it if my master comes out."

I nodded and followed him from stall to stall. Pedro was clearly fond of his charges. He introduced each horse to me by name. Then he offered each animal a handful of grain or a gentle pat. The great beasts tossed their heads and snorted in response.

Then Pedro unlatched one of the stall doors and led a tan-colored horse out. "They are awfully large, are they not?" I asked somewhat nervously. The beast seemed to sense my unease. It gazed at me without blinking and stamped its great feet on the straw-covered floor.

I had had little to do with horses over the course of my life. Mules I understood. Tío Rodrigo, my father's old friend, had always brought his mules when he visited my mother and me. They seemed more predictable than these horses.

"There is nothing to be afraid of," Pedro said. "Horses are wonderful creatures. You just have to be a bit cautious around them until they know you. And it is helpful to know what they like and do not like."

I was sure that Pedro knew what he was talking about. Still, I had no desire to get too close to those huge teeth or heavy hooves.

"Go ahead," Pedro said, "you can pat him if you are careful."

I reached out very slowly to touch the horse. Its dark brown coat felt like velvet under my fingers.

"I think he likes you," announced Pedro, sounding like a proud papa.

I realized that I liked the horse as well. Its dark eyes seemed to overflow with sad secrets. I thought that this animal probably understood loneliness as well as I did.

Apparently Pedro shared the horse's acceptance of me. When I thanked Pedro for the shelter he had provided, he said, "You can come back tonight if you like."

"I will," I said.

After that, my life fell into a pattern. During the daytime, I stayed away from the stables. But every evening, after dark fell, I slipped inside to spend the night. Then, in the morning, I would visit the horses with Pedro. Soon he even allowed me to hold their halters while he groomed their coats.

"You have a way with horses," he said one morning. "I think it is because you tell them stories. They seem to like the sound of your voice."

It was true that I did tell stories to the horses. That may seem silly, but the creatures were a wonderful audience. They stared at me with attentive eyes and never interrupted. So I found myself practicing on them, revising my tales until I was satisfied with the telling. I began to look forward to the time I spent with these enormous yet quiet companions.

Then one day, Pedro woke me long before dawn. “Come!” he said. “I have something wonderful to show you.”

He led me to a stall at the opposite end of the stables. Inside, on a bed of fresh straw, a newborn foal lay next to its mother. As we watched, the mare nudged her baby. The foal struggled to its feet. Moments later, it took a few steps on spindly legs.

I was in awe. It was one of the most marvelous things I had ever experienced. Suddenly I knew what trade I wanted to learn.

Turning to Pedro, I said, “Will you teach me how to be a groom?”

Pedro hesitated for a moment, then nodded. “I will ask the master if I can have an assistant,” he said. “I think he will agree as long as you do not expect to be paid.”

Payment would have been nice. However, I was willing to settle for being able to sleep in the stables without having to sneak in after dark. So Pedro, his master, and I had soon struck a deal.

My initial chores were things I had already helped Pedro do. I brought feed and water to the animals and cleaned their stalls. I did not mind the first task, though the buckets of oats and barley were heavy and awkward to carry. However, cleaning the stalls was less pleasurable. Horses eat a lot. This means there is also a lot to clean up afterward. Still, I was grateful for the job. The more I got to know my charges, the more I liked them.

Pedro and I settled into a comfortable working relationship. He was a good companion, even if he did talk of little else but horses.

One day, finally, I was allowed to take a horse for its exercise. This would be a walk in the long, narrow alley behind the house.

I guess I went about things in the wrong way. As I approached the animal, I was thinking about something else. A story I had heard recently, I believe. Suddenly I heard Pedro cry, "Not from the rear, Diego!"

His warning was almost too late. I had come up behind the horse and startled it. Now the beast kicked out with its rear legs. Thump! The heavy hooves just missed my head. They did *not* miss the gatepost beside me. Splinters of wood had been gouged from the surface.

"Are you all right?" asked Pedro—after checking on the horse and calming it.

"Yes," I said. However, I was shaking from head to foot.

"What were you thinking?" he asked with some heat. "I have told you again and again how you must approach a horse. You never come up behind one! Never!"

I hung my head. "I am sorry," I said. "My mind was on something else."

"Diego, your mind cannot be on *anything* else when you are working with horses."

I sighed. "I do not think I am meant to be a groom, Pedro," I said. "It is far too dangerous a trade for someone whose head is constantly filled with stories."

"I am afraid that you are right," agreed Pedro. "But, Diego, you must have a way to support yourself. Have you thought about becoming a street entertainer? Your stories are wonderful. I have listened as you told them to the horses. I know that other people would be willing to pay a few coins to hear them. Surely you could make a living in such a way."

"Perhaps you are right," I said slowly. "At any rate, I do not know what else I am fit to do."

So that is how I once again found myself

spending my days in the busy marketplace. To be honest, the thought of supporting myself by my stories had crossed my mind more than once. I remembered my attempt to draw an audience for a story shortly after arriving in Seville. I had not been successful then, but I was much wiser in the ways of entertainers now. I was also much cleaner than I had been at that time.

I even knew which were the best spots in the plaza. I just had to wait for one to become vacant. Perhaps a storyteller would tire of Seville and decide to move on to another city, leaving his space open for me. Meanwhile, I claimed a spot at the far edge of the market.

I began with tales I had told often—to the other orphans, to Alonso, and to the horses. They were good tales, I know that. However, my spot was far away from the crowds. I did not earn more than a few coins a day. These I spent on food and rent for a tiny room I had found above a cloth merchant's shop.

When I was not telling stories myself, I was listening to them. I memorized every tale I heard, hoping to someday use it myself. Gradually, I got to know the entertainers who worked in the area regularly. I spent a lot of time with one troupe. It consisted of two couples, one quite old, the other a bit younger. They all worked together to put on plays. However, they each had other talents as well.

Marta and Sancho, the older couple, were husband and wife. Marta was a large woman with gray hair that she tried to hide with dye. Sancho was much skinnier than his wife. He had a shaggy beard that was streaked with white. The two of them were musicians who sang and played a variety of instruments.

The other couple, Manuel and Amelia, were younger. They were a brother-and-sister pair. Manuel sported a head of curly black hair and was a fine juggler. Amelia was dark-haired as well. She was a master puppeteer and also made all the costumes the troupe wore.

They quickly accepted me as one of them and never complained at my constant questions about their art. In fact, they were eager to share what they knew. In his free time, Sancho gave me a few lessons on the pear-shaped rebec, a stringed instrument. But the best I could do was to produce screeching sounds from the instrument.

Manuel offered to teach me how to juggle. However, I did no better than I had the first time I had tried to learn. As soon as I would get two balls in the air, their motion seemed to hypnotize me. I would find myself thinking of a story I wanted to tell and the balls would drop at my feet.

Marta once invited me to sing with her. It was quickly evident that I could not carry a tune, so she never asked again.

I had better luck with Amelia. Her puppet shows were like stories being performed by tiny actors. She showed me how to manipulate the puppets and seemed to appreciate my interest in the stories she told with them.

In a matter of weeks, I came to think of these men and women as my family. I believe that they felt the same way about me.

By now, it was almost December. The days were getting shorter and the nights cooler. I could sense that the troupe was getting restless, so I was not completely surprised when Sancho came to me with an announcement.

"We are leaving Seville tomorrow, Diego," he said. "We plan to head east along the river, working as traveling minstrels. That is usually how we spend our winters."

"I will be sorry to see you go," I said. I meant what I said. I knew that with the troupe gone, I would once again be lonely.

"We wondered if you would care to travel with us," Sancho said.

This I had not expected. My first response was to say no to the offer. Seville was familiar to me now. It was home. Besides, I had not completely given up hope of someday meeting up with Alonso. After all, he would not stay in an orphanage forever. Surely I owed it to my friend to be around in case he came looking for me.

On the other hand, I had to make a living. "What would I be doing?" I asked.

"Amelia says that you could help with the puppets," he responded. "Also, many of our performances have parts for younger actors. They would be better played by you than by one of us. And there are other chores you could do."

All of this sounded promising. Still, I had one more question.

"Will you be returning to Seville in the spring?"

"We always have in the past."

"Then I will come with you," I announced.

X

Life on the Road

"Come one! Come all! There will be a performance in the plaza this afternoon at two o'clock! Come one! Come all!"

As I walked through the streets, I beat a small drum and repeated this message over and over. Doing so before a performance was one of my duties as a member of the traveling company. It was not my favorite job, I admit. Still, if no one knew about the show, no one would attend. And that would mean we earned nothing. So I went on my way, shaking my head frequently to make the bells on my hat jingle merrily. The drum and the bells attracted as much attention as did my words.

For the past month, our journey had taken us through tiny villages and towns. We usually performed in a small tent in whatever space was available. Sometimes our audience consisted of only a few peasants and their children. Other times, we gathered a sizable crowd.

Finally, we arrived at a place with a significant population—the city of Jaén. We set up in the courtyard of a large inn where there was room for our puppet theater. We even had a stage of sorts—made by laying some planks on top of several benches.

"We shall do well here," said Sancho. "There are many guests staying at the inn. All of them will be looking for some entertainment, I am sure. And at this time, we seem to be the only troupe of entertainers in the area."

It appeared that Sancho was right. Spectators began arriving long before two o'clock in hopes of finding a good vantage point. By the time the show began, a large and noisy crowd filled the courtyard.

"I have never seen so many people at one of our performances," I murmured to Marta as we waited to begin. "Do you think they will like the show?"

"I am sure they will," she told me. I hoped she was correct, as unhappy audiences were known to throw vegetables on the stage. I had no desire to be pelted with turnips.

Then the show began. Manuel juggled while I assisted. (My juggling skills had not improved, so my help largely consisted of handing him his equipment.) Marta and Sancho sang several tunes. Then it was time for the puppet show. We put on a performance about a family that fought over olives. The characters were a father, a mother, a daughter, and a neighbor. Because I was the youngest, my role was to do the voice of the daughter. I did not mind this, as no one could see me behind the puppet theater.

Then came my favorite part. The others had agreed that I could tell a story near the end of each performance! I had been very unsure about this at first, but my tales had been well-received. However, because I was nervous about my lack of experience, I only told stories I knew well enough to recite in my sleep.

Marta and Sancho ended our show by playing some lively music. Most of the audience clapped to their tunes, and several people began to dance.

All in all, it was a most satisfactory performance. Especially when Sancho counted the coins that had been dropped into our box. We had enough to pay for a room in the inn and a fine dinner! I was proud that I had done my part toward our success.

We stayed in Jaén for several days, putting on a show every afternoon. However, as often happens, each day our audience got smaller. As a result, so did the money we earned.

"We must move on," Sancho announced after one afternoon's show.

The others agreed, so the next morning found us on the road again. I wished we could have stayed longer. I had liked being in a bustling city again. But now we were back to playing small towns with small audiences.

Not long afterward, things began to go downhill. It was not the fault of any of the members of the troupe. It was the weather that caused our problems. It started to rain. And once the skies opened, it seemed that the rains would never stop.

Of course, no one would come to see a performance in a downpour, even if we were willing to give one. That meant we earned no money. We were forced to eat the food we had carried with us for just such an emergency. Our meals were far from fresh and far from generous.

That was not the worst of it. The mud was everywhere. It coated our shoes and splashed up onto our clothing. And with every turn, the wagon wheels hurled mud into the wagon, so our props and belongings were all wet and dirty.

But the most terrible thing was that we had to sleep in the wagon, all of us stacked like firewood in the small space. The canvas cover was not completely waterproof, so even inside, we were in the rain.

It was understandable that tempers soon began to fray. "Sancho, you snore like an ancient mule," Manuel complained one morning.

"At least Sancho lies still," retorted Marta. "You move all night long, Manuel. As if you were running away on a road that goes nowhere."

"Hah!" retorted Manuel. "If I could run away, I would hardly still be here with you, would I?"

And so it went, day in and day out for almost a week. I felt as if my head would burst with all of the unpleasant things I wanted to say.

However, I kept my mouth shut, as I feared becoming the target of someone else's frustration.

At last I had had enough. Being by myself cannot be any worse than this, I thought. I cleared my throat and waited until everyone had stopped arguing long enough to pay me some attention. "I have decided to return to Seville," I announced.

It is fortunate that I did not expect anyone to try to change my mind. For if I had, I would have been greatly disappointed. I think they were all happy to know they would soon have the small amount of space that my thin body took up.

"When will you leave?" asked Sancho.

"As soon as we arrive at the next town," I said. "Perhaps I will be able to find someone there to travel with me."

He nodded and nothing more was said about the matter. The next morning dawned cloudy, but dry. Everyone's spirits lifted. Perhaps the rains had ended for a time.

Still, now that my decision had been made, I did not want to stay. I was eager to get back to Seville. So as soon as we reached a town, I said my good-byes and left the troupe.

I had learned something from my experience. The life of a traveling entertainer was clearly not the life for me.

XI

I Take a Different Path

I sat on a bench in a small park, trying not to think about the rumbling of my empty stomach. After days of clouds and gloom, the weak sunshine that beat down on me was welcome.

Since leaving the traveling troupe, I had not gone far. Shortly after our parting, I had come down with some sort of illness. (I suppose it was because I had spent so much time being cold and wet.) For several days, I had hidden away in a pile of straw stacked high behind a stable in this small town. All I had done was sleep.

My fever had broken at last. But I was still weak, and I was very hungry. I realized that I did not have enough strength to walk to the next town, let alone all the way to Seville.

So I sat, wondering what was to become of me.

Then a voice not too far away drew my attention. "What shall we do?" it asked.

I looked up. At the edge of the road that passed the park, a pair of well-dressed gentlemen stood and stared at a carriage drawn by a beautiful black horse. A wheel had slipped off, I saw. The carriage tipped to one side dangerously.

I watched as the men unharnessed the horse and tied its reins to a post. Next they walked around the carriage—first one way, then the other. Finally, the taller of the two said, "I will lift the carriage and you can slip the wheel back into place."

This was no solution, I knew. For even from here, I could see that the axle itself was cracked. Surely they would notice.

They did not. With much huffing and puffing, the first gentleman lifted one end of the carriage. The second slipped the wheel into place. Then the carriage was lowered. The axle gave way, and the wheel slipped off again.

The taller gentleman pulled a handkerchief from his pocket. As he did so, I saw something fall to the ground.

I rose to my feet slowly and walked toward them. "Excuse me, sir," I said, "but you dropped something. And I must tell you that your carriage has a broken axle. It will have to be fixed before you can replace the wheel."

The tall man immediately reached down to pick up what he had dropped—a folded paper, I noted. He stuffed it back into his pocket, then turned toward me.

I half expected him to shoo me away, for I knew I was dirty and probably smelled like someone who had slept behind a stable.

Instead, the man said, "Thank you." Then he removed his hat and scratched his head. "I am sure you are right about the carriage. For my part, I know nothing about things like axles."

I was astounded. How could one be fortunate enough to have a carriage and know nothing about axles?

"I told you we should have hired another coachman after ours fell ill," the short gentleman said. Then he looked at me. "Perhaps you can assist us, boy. Do you know where we might find someone who could repair the axle?"

"I am sorry, sir," I said, "but I am a stranger here myself. However, there is a stable not far down the road. I am sure that someone there could help you."

The two men conferred for a few moments. I could not hear what they said, but before long, the short gentleman addressed me. "Can you show us where it is?" he asked.

I wondered how hard they thought it could be to find a stable in such a small town. However, I nodded and agreed to take them there.

As we walked, the taller gentleman said, "Allow us to introduce ourselves. I am Hernando de Vega, and this is my brother, Federico. We are silk merchants on our way home to Toledo."

He finished speaking and waited, obviously expecting me to introduce myself in return.

"I am pleased to meet you, Don Hernando and Don Federico," I said. I found myself speaking more formally than was usually my habit. It was obvious that these men were prosperous and well-educated. "I am Diego . . . Diego de Granada," I continued.

It was the first time I had given myself that name. I suddenly felt that it was not enough to call myself simply "Diego" as I had been doing. I was now more than 12 years old, after all—practically a man. And, as I said before, I liked the sound of "Granada." It seemed grand.

"I see," said Don Hernando. "You said you are a stranger in this village. I assume then, that you come from Granada."

"That is where I was born," I admitted.

"So you are traveling with your parents." He made this a statement rather than a question, so

I did not respond. I suspected that he was making fun of me. From my appearance, he had to know that I was on my own.

Suddenly I began to worry and wished I had never approached the gentlemen. Would they take me to the authorities, thinking I was a runaway?

However, nothing more was said about the matter. Instead, the two men discussed things such as how long it might take to get the axle fixed and what they would do when they reached their home in Toledo.

I paused when we were close to the stable. "There it is," I said. "I am sure you can get help with your problem."

"Thank you, Diego," said Don Hernando. "And once that is taken care of, perhaps we can help you with yours as well."

"Wh-wh-what do you mean?" I stammered.

"I may be mistaken, Diego, but I think that you are traveling alone. It is dangerous for a boy of your tender years to do so."

When I made no response, he continued. "When we first met, you were honest enough to tell me that I had dropped something. That paper is an important contract, and it would not have been good for our business had I lost it. You also came to our aid about the axle. So we do not care to leave you here and forever wonder what became of you."

As he spoke, he looked toward his brother, who nodded. Then they both turned to me. The kindness in their eyes was my undoing. I found myself telling the truth. "I am an orphan," I confessed. "I have been traveling with a troupe of entertainers, but that was not working out. So I decided to strike out on my own and return to Seville. That is where I had been living."

"Is someone waiting for you in Seville?" asked Don Hernando.

"Not exactly," I murmured.

"Well, then, we have a proposal for you," he said. "Do you think you can drive our carriage?"

I had to ponder this question for a moment. It was tempting to say yes, but to be truthful, I was not sure. My experience with horses had not included anything as fine as driving a carriage.

"I do not know," I admitted. "I have never done so. But I have worked with mules and horses before."

"We appreciate your honesty," Don Hernando said. "And you are probably better qualified to drive this carriage than either of us. So what do you say? Would you like to hire on as our driver?

It would get you to Toledo, and there are many opportunities there for a boy like you."

It did not take me long to come to a decision. I knew that in my present condition, I would never make it back to Seville on foot. Here was a chance to travel by carriage, like a fine gentleman. Even if I did have to learn to drive it first.

"I would like that very much," I said.

"Then let us get the carriage fixed and be on our way," Don Federico said.

So that is how I found myself driving a coach. Fortunately, I had no problem managing the horse, which was obviously intelligent and well-trained. (The two gentleman let me practice guiding the coach around the park several times—while they stood and watched from a safe distance.)

I must say that riding is certainly a far more pleasant way to travel than is walking. It is far faster as well. Of course, we could not go the entire distance in one day. When it began to grow dark, the gentlemen directed me to stop at an inn. I was given a bed in the stable, but at least this time I had a blanket to wrap myself in. And I went to bed with a full stomach.

We traveled this way for several days, eventually arriving in Toledo. This city is also on a river—though not the same river that flows through Seville. Toledo is smaller in size than Seville, with a population to match. However, it boasts a great cathedral that took over 200 years to complete. Its tower is a truly impressive sight and is visible from a great distance outside the city.

In Toledo, the brothers lived in identical houses, each with its own courtyard and fountain. In between, a coach house separated the two residences.

"You are welcome to sleep in the coach house, Diego," Don Federico told me. "At least until you have found a way to make a living."

"And you can count on a meal each evening from one or the other of us," added Don Hernando. "Simply come around to the back. We will tell our cooks that you are to be fed."

I was touched by their generosity. After all, they hardly knew me and had no obligation toward me. I counted my blessings in meeting up with such good people.

The next day, I headed for the marketplace. As is usual, it was a busy area of the city. I walked everywhere and observed everything. How shall I make my living? I wondered.

The brothers actually helped me with this decision as well. That evening, while I was eating a meal in the courtyard at the back of Don Hernando's house, he approached me.

"Ah, Diego, I was hoping to find you here. I wonder if you could do a task for me tomorrow."

"Of course, sir. I would be happy to."

"Very well, I have a bolt of silk that must be delivered to a customer."

So that is how I began my career as a messenger and courier. I often carried things for Don Hernando and Don Federico. Their clients hired me in turn. Soon I was able to earn enough to allow me to pay rent on a small room not far from the marketplace. However, I still returned frequently to the home of one or the other of the brothers to eat and to visit.

I tried to do my job well, and my reputation as an honest worker grew. Packages and notes in hand, I went from weaver to tailor to leather crafter to shoemaker to jeweler to baker to butcher to barber to scribe to lawyer to blacksmith to glassblower. Before long I knew every nook and cranny of the city. And most of Toledo's merchants and craftspeople as well.

"Ah, Diego," a client would say. "It is good to have a dependable person to rely upon. Here is a coin to take this package to its destination."

My head was no longer in the clouds, as the baker had said so long ago. I could not afford to let myself be distracted. I had learned that making a living is a serious business.

However, while my head was filled with business, my heart was filled with stories. I recited them to myself and to the servants at Don Hernando's and Don Federico's.

I must also tell you about one of the truly wonderful discoveries I made while living in Toledo—the public bathhouse. There were dozens of these buildings all over the city.

One of the best things about the bathhouses was that anyone could use them. Young or old, rich or poor, man or woman—it did not matter. Of course, in most cases, men and women used different bathhouses. Or, if they used the same, they did so on alternate days.

I tried several different bathhouses. They were all more or less the same. Each had three halls. First you would go into what was known as the "cold hall." It was long and narrow and unheated. Here you removed your clothing and put on a dressing gown and a pair of wooden shoes.

In the middle hall, there was a pool and a water fountain. The high, domed roof featured beautiful windows of colored glass. The room was pleasantly heated by hot air pipes in the walls.

The last hall was called the "hot chamber." Here hot water was poured on the floor to make steam. Then, after washing, you would step into a tub that had taps for hot and cold water. It was all heavenly—especially for someone who had not had many baths in his life.

But my real reason for mentioning the bathhouses is that I made a good friend at one of them. It was a lady who worked there. Her name was Maria. She and her husband were plumbers who took care of the pipes. I was curious about how everything worked, so naturally I stopped to ask questions. That had led to our friendship.

One day Maria said to me, "Diego, you appear to be a very smart boy. I know from talking to you that you are interested in almost everything. That you want to learn about every subject you can.

"It is none of my business, of course," she continued. "Still, it seems that you could do more than run errands and deliver packages."

"I do not mind the work," I said. And it was true. In general, I was quite satisfied with my life in Toledo. I was able to pay my rent and to eat regularly. I could afford the small fee charged at the bathhouse whenever I wanted to go. And when I needed company, I could visit with Don Hernando, Don Federico, or any of the other friends I had made. All in all, there was nothing too terribly wrong with things as they were.

"That may be so," Maria said. "However, I think you are wasting a fine mind."

Her words bothered me a little, I must admit. After that conversation, I found myself thinking more often about my future. Would I be able to live forever on what I could earn as a courier? What about Seville, the city I most loved? Would I ever have enough money to get back there, even if only for a visit? And there was Alonso to consider as well. Perhaps he had left the orphanage and gone in search of me.

All of these questions left me somewhat less contented than I had been.

Then one day, Maria brought up the subject again. "Diego, I have heard from my cousin, who is a lawyer. He is looking for an assistant. Someone to be a scribe and secretary. I told him about you, and he would like to meet you. I think you should consider this opportunity."

I thought it over. Surely it would do no harm to talk to the gentleman. "Where should I meet him?" I asked.

"He lives in Seville."

My decision was made. I was on my way back to Seville.

My Return to Seville

Seville had not changed much since I had last seen it. Of course, that was not really surprising. After all, I had been gone less than a year.

I was glad to be back. The trip had been long and tiring. Fortunately, I had been able to ride in a coach with a merchant friend of Don Hernando's. Otherwise, I might still be on the road.

My first destination upon arriving was Don Eduardo's bakery.

"Diego!" my old friend cried. "You have returned! It is good to see you. How are you?"

"I am very well, Don Eduardo," I said. I was pleased to see that the same could be said about the baker. His shop looked prosperous and he seemed content.

"Here," he said with his customary generosity, "have a roll. They just came from the oven."

"I will," I said. "And I can pay for it now, Don Eduardo."

The two of us talked for a while. Don Eduardo was interested in all that had happened to me. "You have a way with words, Diego," he said, "and your life is as interesting as any of the tales told by the storytellers."

When we parted, I promised to come back. Then I headed for the oldest part of Seville, on the left bank of the river. I walked through the narrow, twisting streets of the old city. It had rained that morning, so the cobblestone pavement was slippery.

At last I found the residence I was seeking. Don Alvaro Castillo, the lawyer, lived in an apartment on the second floor of an old house. I went up the steps and knocked at the door.

It opened to reveal a middle-aged man. He was average in physical appearance, though a bit taller and thinner than some. His coal-black hair was slicked back from a high forehead, and he was dressed in what I took to be the latest fashion.

"Yes?" he said, looking down at me with a superior air.

"My name is Diego de Granada," I responded. "I have come from Toledo to apply for the position of secretary."

"Ah, yes," he said. "My cousin Maria said that you would come. Well, come in, boy. We will discuss the matter."

I entered, curious to see the inside of the apartment. It was richly furnished, as I would have guessed from the way Don Alvaro dressed. But the best part was the books. They filled three shelves—more books than I had ever seen in one location before. (Other than in a library, of course. And I had only been to such a place once in my life.)

The building had an interior courtyard, so the apartment featured a balcony that faced inside rather than toward the street. The courtyard was a colorful sight, filled with green plants and bright flowers.

Don Alvaro asked a few questions. Mainly he wanted to be sure that I truly could read and write. Once that was established, the rest of our discussion consisted of Don Alvaro talking while I listened.

"I need the services of a scribe and secretary," he began. "My cousin probably told you that I have a law degree from one of the finest universities in all of Europe. So I am a very busy man whose services are in great demand."

I nodded and tried to look properly impressed. However, I admit that when he went on to talk of his many accomplishments, my mind wandered a bit.

Then he said something that could not fail to catch my attention. "Of course, I am also looking for someone who will be suitable to accompany me when I receive my royal appointment to the Indies. I am expecting that to happen any day now."

The Indies! Could it be possible? I had dreamed of going there ever since hearing Brother Joseph's stories of explorers and traders and their voyages across the sea. Perhaps my dream was going to come true at last!

"So, Diego, I am willing to give you a try," Don Alvaro concluded. He went on to talk of the terms of my employment. These were not overly precise, but I did not care. All that mattered was the possibility that this job might actually take me over the sea and to the Indies.

"I will do my best to be a good employee," I said when he was finally done talking.

So my next career began—my work as a scribe and secretary. I soon found that I was well-suited to the job. I loved the idea of putting pen to paper, even if much of what Don Alvaro had me do was to take down his life story. He was sure that someone would want to read it someday.

But the best part of the job was having access

to my master's book collection. "You may read whenever your duties allow you sufficient time, Diego," he told me. "After all, it is in my best interests to see that you are well-informed. Especially about life and customs in the Indies."

Naturally, I greeted this news with excitement. I read whenever I was not sleeping or busy with other duties.

In addition to my secretarial chores, I was responsible for taking care of Don Alvaro's clothing, making his bed, and similar household tasks. None of this was exactly what I had expected, but the books more than made up for it.

Now and then Don Alvaro would be approached to draw up a contract or a deed. I would go with him to meet with a client. Then we would come home and I would record what he dictated, using my best handwriting.

This was all very interesting, but such things did not happen often. I soon realized that my master did not *need* to work. His family had been rich forever, it seemed. So he had more money than he could spend. I found this hard to believe, but apparently it was so.

To tell the truth, it was fortunate that my master was wealthy. Don Alvaro did not seem interested in seeking out work—or in anything that had to do with the present. He was far more concerned about what lay ahead. That suited me, I will admit. After all, the future included a voyage to the Indies!

Because of this interest, he spent a lot of time near the House of Trade, where the sailing dates and routes of sailings are scheduled. There he could talk to merchants who had invested money in ships that traveled to and from the Indies. They would discuss the prices of silver and gold and the market for exotic goods brought back to Spain from the New World. I listened to their conversations carefully, storing information away for the time when I would find myself in that wondrous land.

However, month followed month and still nothing had come of our proposed voyage. Don Alvaro talked of it constantly, but I began to wonder if the "royal appointment" he was waiting for would ever happen.

In fact, during all this time, the closest I came to the New World was a trip I took to the printer's shop. Don Alvaro sent me there to pick up a book he had ordered. When I entered the shop, the first thing I saw was a large book lying open on a table. There was no one else in the shop—even the owner was not in sight. So, thinking to satisfy my curiosity as I waited, I moved closer to examine the volume. It was lovely, with pages in pure white, punctuated by the black type. The binding was of leather in a beautiful shade of gray. The subject matter, too, was interesting. The book was a traveler's account of his time in New Spain.

"I see you are interested in that book," a voice said. "It was just returned from the bookbinder today."

I looked up and met the bright eyes of an gray-haired gentleman. "I am Don Florencio," he said. "And you are . . . ?"

"I am Diego de Granada," I answered. "Secretary to Don Alvaro. I came to pick up the book he ordered."

"Ah, yes," said Don Florencio. "He is still talking of traveling to the Indies, apparently. Is that why you were studying this book?"

"Partly, sir," I answered. "But also because it is so beautiful. I have never seen such fine work."

Don Florencio seemed pleased by the compliment. He went on to explain in great detail the process by which the book had been printed and bound. I was fascinated by all that he told me and asked many questions.

At last he said, "I have run on enough, my boy. Don Alvaro will be wondering what has become of you."

He gave me the book my master had ordered. And then he invited me to come back any time I wanted to talk about books or how they were printed.

When I arrived back at Don Alvaro's apartment, I apologized for taking so long.

"I understand," he said, waving one hand in the air. "Don Florencio is a terrible bore, is he not? The man goes on and on and on about printing to anyone who will listen. I am merely grateful that this time *you* had to listen to him and not I."

I could not understand how Don Alvaro could find Don Florencio boring, but I kept my thoughts to myself.

I had found that in the evenings, Don Alvaro appreciated my company. For all his riches, I think that he was a lonely man. Whether that was true or not, he seemed glad to have someone else around. He talked far more than I did. This did not bother me because I learned a great deal by listening to him.

Then one evening, Don Alvaro said, "You should know how to play chess, Diego. I could teach you."

"I would like that, sir," I responded. I knew a little bit about the game. I had watched chess matches that were played in the plaza. It seemed an interesting and complex activity.

"Some call chess the 'royal game' because kings and emperors have played it through the ages," Don Alvaro explained. "Personally, I find it a worthy game because it requires imagination, concentration, and the ability to anticipate events. In other words, Diego, it is a game of strategy and decisions. Much like life itself.

"Come," he continued. "There is no reason why you should not have your first lesson tonight." He opened the door to a cupboard and took out a chessboard and a dark wooden box.

"This particular set belonged to my grandfather," he said as he reached into the box and began removing the playing pieces. "He taught me the game when I was much younger than you. He predicted that with my intelligence, I would become a great player. In all modesty, I think he was right. So I will now teach you." He proceeded to place the chess pieces on the board, giving the name and function of each as he did so.

My head swam. I could not keep the pieces themselves straight, let alone the moves that they could or could not make. King or knight, pawn or castle—they were all the same to me. Don Alvaro became a bit impatient. "You are a bright boy, Diego. You should be able to master the game," he said. "We will have another lesson tomorrow night, after we finish our dinner."

"Yes, sir," I said. However, I suspected that he would soon lose interest in trying to teach me the game. For my part, I was not sure that I was capable of mastering it to his satisfaction!

However, he seemed determined to teach me. Or perhaps he just liked having an opponent readily available. Whatever the reason, we worked at chess every evening for weeks.

By the end of that time, I was pleased to realize that the game was finally beginning to make sense to me. Of course, I was no match for Don Alvaro, who had been playing for years. But at least I was now making him work a little harder for his triumphs.

One evening, about half an hour after we had started a match, he sat and studied the board for a long time. "You are improving, Diego," he said at last.

"Thank you, sir. As you told me, chess is truly a marvelous game."

"Yes, it is," he said thoughtfully. He pondered his next move for at least ten minutes. After that, the game was over quickly. He was the winner, of course.

Two weeks later, however, something most

unusual happened. We were in the middle of a match when I realized something. I could counter any move Don Alvaro might make. He could not win this game!

Three more moves and Don Alvaro came to the same conclusion. “It is a draw,” he said. “We are tied.”

I waited for his praise. Instead, he said, “Perhaps I am coming down with a cold. Certainly I was not playing my best tonight.”

After that, we played to a tie on several more occasions. Each time, Don Alvaro seemed upset by the results. I should have known then what was going to happen, but I was not smart enough to see it.

One night we played long after dark. The candles cast their wavering light over the board. Suddenly I became excited. In my mind, I could map out every move that I would make. And I could see every move Don Alvaro could possibly make in response. There was no way he could defeat me. I was going to win the game!

I held my breath, hoping I had not been wrong. Then, three more moves and the game was almost mine. "Check," I said. And, after his next move, "Checkmate." The game was over. There was nothing Don Alvaro could do.

He studied the board for a long time. Then he swept the pieces from it, scattering them on the floor. This was not the reaction I had anticipated.

"Was I mistaken, sir?" I asked.

"No," he said shortly. He left the room without

another word. Puzzled, I picked up the pieces and put them away.

I guess I should not have learned the game so well. The next morning, Don Alvaro informed me that he no longer needed my services.

I knew I had done nothing wrong. I knew that I had been a loyal and efficient secretary. However, I have my pride. I did not beg for my job. I simply left. I remembered something my mother had always said: "When one door closes, another one opens."

Besides, I was quite sure that Don Alvaro was never going to get his royal appointment to the Indies. Ten years in the future, he would still be talking about how it would happen "any day now."

I was going to have to take charge of my life without him. And I knew exactly what I wanted to do.

XIII
The Present

This time, I did not wander the streets wondering what was to become of me. I had a plan. I took myself straight to the shop of Don Florencio, the printer.

I had visited the kindly old gentleman several times after our first meeting, and he had always been glad to see me. Once he had even let me help him set some words into type. It had seemed magical when I saw those words transferred on to paper!

"Welcome, Diego," he said when I entered. "I was wondering when I might see you again. Have you come just to visit, or does Don Alvaro want something printed?"

"Neither," I answered. "I have come to ask a favor, Don Florencio. A very large favor."

He wiped his hands on his apron to remove the ink, then gestured toward the door at the back of the shop. I knew that this was where his living quarters were, though I had never been in that part of the building.

A few minutes later, we were both seated comfortably. “Now, tell me about this favor,” Don Florencio urged.

“I am in need of a job,” I explained. “Don Alvaro has let me go.”

“That is hard to believe,” the old printer said. “He has always spoken very highly of your abilities. He told me once that you were a very bright young man who would do well.”

“Well, he no longer seems to feel that way,” I said. I explained what had happened.

Don Florencio began to laugh. "Ah, yes, apparently you are *too* bright, Diego. Don Alvaro considers himself a masterful chess player. I do not suppose he took too kindly to being defeated by a mere student of the game."

Then he became more serious. "How can I help you with a job, Diego? I assume you are still interested in sailing to the Indies, with or without Don Alvaro. I know several officers on some of the merchant ships that sail from Seville. Do you want me to write a letter of recommendation to one of them? I would be happy to do so."

Suddenly I was nervous. What if Don Florencio said no to my request. "Actually, I had something else in mind," I said. The rest of my words came out in a rush. I told him that I liked everything about his shop—the smell of the ink, the noise of the great printing press, the feel of the type in my fingers.

Suddenly I stopped talking and looked down at my hands, which were clasped so tightly that my knuckles had turned white. I finished in a quiet voice. "I was wondering if you would be willing to take me on as your apprentice."

For what seemed like an eternity, the room was quiet. I wished that I could disappear. Clearly, Don Florencio had no interest in my services.

"Diego," he said at last. That was it, just my name.

I looked up. The old gentleman was smiling. "I would be proud to have you as an apprentice," he said.

"Do you mean it? I will work so hard, Don Florencio. I promise."

"I have no doubt of that, Diego," he said. "I have two sons, you know. I dearly wanted one or both of them to learn my trade and take over the business some day. But they were not interested. The lure of adventure was too much for them. They are both captains in the Indies. I have not seen either one of them for over two years."

So that is how I came to be a printer's apprentice. I have been with Don Florencio for several months now. I am as excited by the work today as I was when I first visited the shop.

This makes sense, I am sure you will agree. After all, what is printing but storytelling at its finest? Every book we produce spins a tale of some kind. Some are true and others are made up, but all are stories.

And that is not all. I have told Don Florencio about Alonso. He says that he will ask around to find out if my friend is still in an orphanage. If so, he will tell Alonso to come and find us when he strikes out on his own.

As for my dream of seeing the Indies—I have not given up on that. Don Florencio has even hinted that he might someday travel to the New World with me. He would be closer to his sons, he says. And we could open a print shop there.

Whatever happens, I—Diego de Granada—will welcome the adventure.

The History Behind Diego's Story

Diego de Granada is an account of several years in the life of a fictional boy of 16th century Spain. The story also explains other aspects of one of the most exciting periods in Spanish history—a time not long after Christopher Columbus claimed a "New World" for King Ferdinand and Queen Isabella.

It is a well-known fact that Columbus mistakenly believed he had achieved his goal of reaching India. That is why the natives of the lands he first explored were called *Indians.* It is also why that part of the world is still known as the West Indies. These Caribbean islands were the first areas explored, conquered, and colonized by Spain.

In 1516, King Ferdinand and Queen Isabella's grandson, sixteen-year-old Carlos, became the new king of Spain. He ruled over a great empire. It included Spain and its territories in the Indies plus the Netherlands, Germany, and parts of Italy and North Africa.

Twice a year, large fleets of Spanish ships would set sail for Spain from the New World, loaded down with precious cargo. The ships traveled together to avoid pirates from other countries. Most Spanish ships returned to home ports in Cádiz or Seville. By law, one-fifth of the cargo they carried back to Spain belonged to Carlos. This share of the riches was known as "the king's fifth." The remainder of the treasure eventually traveled far and wide to other parts of the "Old World."

Seville became the most splendid and prosperous of Spain's port cities. It was there that the important business of the New World was conducted until the Spanish colonies in the New World became independent.

Today, the influence of Spain can still be seen in the countries where Spanish sailors once traveled. In many of those countries, Spanish is the native language of the majority of the people. In addition, King Carlos' fleets brought unfamiliar foods to the New World—things like wheat, bananas, oranges, rice, and coffee. The natives of these countries, in turn, introduced the Old World to foods that were native to the new one—tomatoes, potatoes, corn, pineapples, chocolate, and vanilla, for example.

Centuries after Diego's story takes place, Seville is still beautiful. The same narrow cobblestone streets and charming neighborhoods that he describes are still there. But along the Guadalquivir River, there are no longer ships loading goods destined for the New World—or unloading treasures for the Old World. The city is alive and well, but the hustle and bustle of the port is gone.